HERGÉ

THE ADVENTURES OF TINTIN

THE CASTAFIORE EMERALD

The TINTIN books are published in the following languages :

Afrikaans :		HUMAN & ROUSSEAU, Cape Town.
Arabic :		DAR AL-MAAREF, Cairo.
Basque :		MENSAJERO, Bilbao.
Brazilian :		DISTRIBUIDORA RECORD, Rio de Janeiro.
Breton :		CASTERMAN, Paris.
Catalan :		JUVENTUD, Barcelona.
Chinese :		EPOCH, Taipei.
Danish :		CARLSEN IF, Copenhagen.
Dutch :		CASTERMAN, Dronten.
English :	U.K. :	METHUEN CHILDREN'S BOOKS, London.
	Australia :	REED PUBLISHING AUSTRALIA, Melbourne.
	Canada :	REED PUBLISHING CANADA, Toronto.
	New Zealand :	REED PUBLISHING NEW ZEALAND, Auckland.
	Republic of South Africa :	STRUIK BOOK DISTRIBUTORS, Johannesburg.
	Singapore :	REED PUBLISHING ASIA, Singapore.
	Spain :	EDICIONES DEL PRADO, Madrid.
	Portugal :	EDICIONES DEL PRADO, Madrid.
	U.S.A.	LITTLE BROWN, Boston.
Esperanto :		CASTERMAN, Paris.
Finnish :		OTAVA, Helsinki.
French :		CASTERMAN, Paris-Tournai.
	Spain :	EDICIONES DEL PRADO, Madrid.
	Portugal :	EDICIONES DEL PRADO, Madrid.
Galician :		JUVENTUD, Barcelona.
German :		CARLSEN, Reinbek-Hamburg.
Greek :		ANGLO-HELLENIC, Athens.
Icelandic :		FJÖLVI, Reykjavik.
Indonesian :		INDIRA, Jakarta.
Iranian :		MODERN PRINTING HOUSE, Teheran.
Italian :		GANDUS, Genoa.
Japanese :		FUKUINKAN SHOTEN, Tokyo.
Korean :		UNIVERSAL PUBLICATIONS, Seoul.
Malay :		SHARIKAT UNITED, Pulau Pinang.
Norwegian :		SEMIC, Oslo.
Picard :		CASTERMAN, Paris.
Portuguese :		CENTRO DO LIVRO BRASILEIRO, Lisboa.
Provençal :		CASTERMAN, Paris.
Spanish :		JUVENTUD, Barcelona.
	Argentina :	JUVENTUD ARGENTINA, Buenos Aires.
	Mexico :	MARIN, Mexico.
	Peru :	DISTR. DE LIBROS DEL PACIFICO, Lima.
Serbo-Croatian :		DECJE NOVINE, Gornji Milanovac.
Swedish :		CARLSEN IF, Stockholm.
Welsh :		GWASG Y DREF WEN, Cardiff.

Translated by Leslie Lonsdale-Cooper
and Michael Turner

First published in Great Britain in 1963.
Published as a paperback in 1973 by Methuen Children's Books Ltd.
Reprinted 1975, 1977 and 1978
Magnet edition reprinted seven times
Reissued 1989 by Mammoth,
an imprint of Reed Consumer Books Ltd
Michelin House, 81 Fulham Road, London SW3 6RB
and Auckland, Melbourne, Singapore and Toronto
Reprinted 1990, 1991, 1992, 1993 (twice), 1994, 1995, 1996, 1997, 1998 , 1999 , 2001
Printed in Belgium by Casterman Printers s.a., Tournai
ISBN 0-7497-0169-2

THE CASTAFIORE EMERALD

Ah, the merry month of May!... Spring, the sweet spring ♫ Cuckoo, jug-jug, pu-we, to-witta-woo!

The chorus of birds... the woodland flowers... the fragrant perfumes... the sweet-smelling earth! Breathe deeply, Tintin. Fill your lungs with fresh air... air so pure and sparkling you could drink it!

As far as perfume goes, I wouldn't call this exactly fragrant.

You're right!

No wonder! Look at that disgusting rubbish dump. The filth from every dustbin in the neighbourhood is chucked over there.

Good heavens! Some people seem to be attracted by the stink! ... Fantastic!

Gipsies!

No sense of hygiene, the guttersnipes. Incredible!

Ssh!... Listen! That sounds like a child crying ...

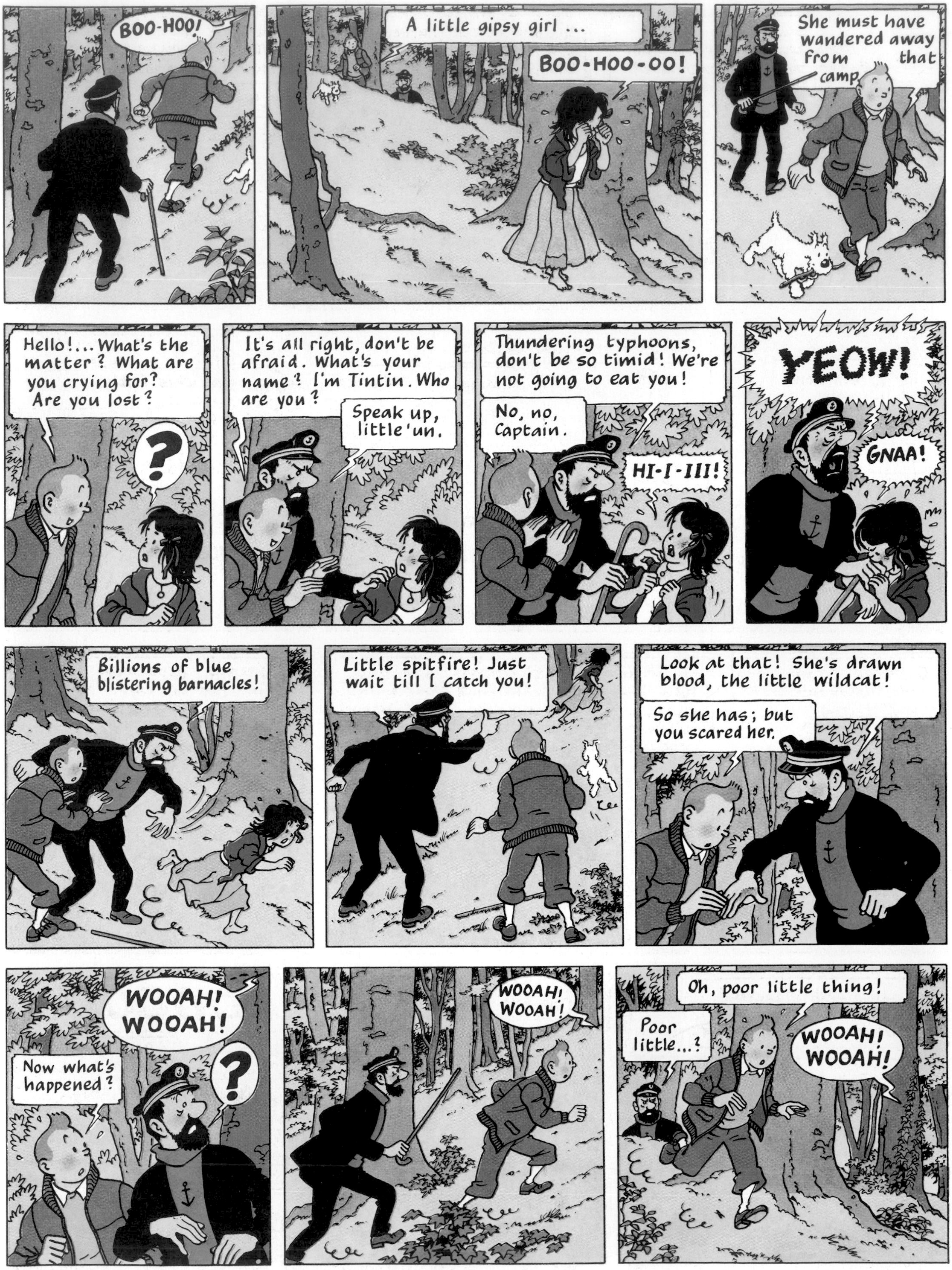
BOO-HOO!
A little gipsy girl ...
BOO-HOO-OO!
She must have wandered away from that camp.
Hello!... What's the matter? What are you crying for? Are you lost?
?
It's all right, don't be afraid. What's your name? I'm Tintin. Who are you?
Speak up, little'un.
Thundering typhoons, don't be so timid! We're not going to eat you!
No, no, Captain.
HI-I-III!
YEOW!
GNAA!
Billions of blue blistering barnacles!
Little spitfire! Just wait till I catch you!
Look at that! She's drawn blood, the little wildcat!
So she has; but you scared her.
WOOAH! WOOAH!
Now what's happened?
?
WOOAH! WOOAH!
Oh, poor little thing!
Poor little...?
WOOAH! WOOAH!

Good gracious! She tripped over the brambles and then bumped her head on the tree-root.

You haven't cut yourself, have you?... No, there isn't any blood. I expect you'll have a bump, that's all.

Little goose!

Please, don't be frightened. We'll take you back to your mother... Can you stand up?

KILIKILIKILI!

O.K. now?

A few minutes later...

Mama!

Miarka!

To think that people live in the midst of all this filth!

I know.

Good day to you!

We found her in the woods; she must have wandered off. When she saw us she...er... she ran away. But then she fell over and bumped her head on a tree root. So we brought her home.

You are a good man. I will tell your fortune. You cross my palm with silver!

No, thanks. Definitely not!

Er... It might be as well, for a clear conscience, to let a doctor have a look at her.

A doctor! I suppose you think we have money to pay for a doctor!

Kind gentleman! I'll tell your fortune... you cross my palm with silver...

No, no! Please leave me alone!

OOOOOH!

What is it?... Tell me!

Trouble!

Well, if that's all you can see, I can tell your fortune, too!

You must be careful...otherwise I see an accident... But not serious ...I see you in a carriage...AAAH! A beautiful stranger approaches... She is coming to visit you...AAAH! She has wonderful jewels, and... OOH!...A terrible disaster...

Go on, go on!

The jewels are gone... vanished!...stolen! You cross my palm with silver and I tell you many more things.

No, no! That's enough! Let go of my hand!

Just a little silver...otherwise you will suffer great misfortune! ...The jewels will disappear!

Me too!...That's enough mumbo-jumbo for one day.

Well, goodbye, and take care of that little cherub. But if you take my advice, you'll camp somewhere else, and not on this rubbish-dump... In the first place, it's unhealthy...

D'you think we're here because we like it? D'you imagine we enjoy living surrounded by filth?

You mean...

Quiet, Mike, let me talk to this gajo.

Me, a gajo?

That's what we call anyone who isn't a Romany... Listen, we arrived here yesterday with a sick man, and this was the only place where the police would let us camp.

So that's it!

Blistering barnacles! Now, just you listen to me. You're not staying here!...There's a large meadow near the Hall, beside a stream. You can move in there whenever you like.

Making people live on a dung-heap like this. It's revolting!

I'm glad you could help them.

THUMP

Poor Professor!... Anything broken?

Yes, a piece several inches long!

That confounded step! Still not repaired! When's that sluggard of a builder coming?

I telephone him constantly, sir, and he assures me he'll come...

Well, I'll show you how to deal with him!

Hello?... Hello? Mr. Bolt?... What, that isn't Mr. Bolt?

No, sir, this is Cutts the butcher ...Yes, sir, ... Not at all, sir.

CRASH

Hello?... Is that Mr. Bolt?

Yes...oh, yes sir...Yes, I do know...I...Yes, a sudden rush of work...Yes, very tiresome...What? Oh yes, sir, it's very dangerous too...When? ...Well, yes, I...I'll come along...er...tomorrow. Yes, first thing tomorrow...You can rely on me, sir. Good-bye.

That's how to get results, Nestor. Just a touch of firmness, that's all. He'll be here tomorrow, as you heard.

Seeing is believing, sir!

Now for a little drink : the fresh air makes me thirsty!... All well, Tintin?

A letter from Chang in London : he's fine, and sends you his regards.

What a nice lad he is.

Yes, and another letter...You'll never guess who from: Bianca Castafiore!

Bianca Castafiore! Ha! ha! ha! The dear old Milanese nightingale!

AAAAAH ♪♪
My beauty...

SPLOTCH

...past compare... ♪ Ma-a-a-argarita ♪♪

Hello, there's a storm brewing.

And what has that delightful creature to say?

No, it's passed over.

That she's arriving here at Marlinspike tomorrow!

Castafiore?... Tomorrow??... Here??? You're pulling my leg!!!

Read it yourself.

My dear young Tintin, it is so long since... blablabla... two recitals in your country... blablabla... escape from the press... blablabla... May your simple and unaffected friend (not half!) invite herself to Marlinspike Hall?... blabla-bla... I shall arrive on the 17th... What?

Castafiore?!... Here!?... Cataclysm! Calamity! Catastrophe!

Er... there's a little postscript for you...

Kindest regards to Captain Bartok.

Haddock, by thunder, Signora Castoroili!... Haddock!

NESTOR!

Coming, sir!

Nestor, pack my bags this instant! I must be out of this house in an hour!

Very good... sir...

It's no good protesting: I'm weighing anchor!

THUMP

Er... it's the step, sir.

But, thundering typhoons, you knew the step was broken!... I've made myself hoarse reminding you about it!

Er... yes, sir... The doorbell, sir.

DONG

I'll go. You get on with my packing.

Pity he's going; the fur would really fly with Castafiore here...

MRRAW

A telegram for you Tintin. Who knows: perhaps Bianca Cataclysm is held up.

Well?

It's from her, all right!

6

Sincere regrets. Stop. Cannot come...

Splendid!

HOORAY!

!

Good gracious me, I shouldn't have come without my umbrella.

Happy day! She isn't coming, Cuthbert old friend!

No, but I don't suppose it will last.

But...

Nestor!...Nestor! You can stop packing! I shan't be going!

That isn't all, Captain...

Er...very good, sir.

Sincere regrets. Stop. Cannot come 17th. Stop. Arriving 16th. Stop. Regards, Bianca.

WHAT?!

The 16th!...The 16th!... But it's the 16th today!

Exactly, Captain.

All hands on deck! Abandon ship! Every man for himself! I'm off!

But where?

I don't know! Doesn't matter where. Milan perhaps. I've never dared go there in case I met that thundering typhoon!

But...

Nestor!...Nestor!...My bags! ...At once!

CRRUMP THUMP BUMP

?

Captain! Captain!

Billions of bilious blue blistering barnacles!

Thundering typhoons, that step!... That confounded step! Just wait till I see that bone-idle builder!

Nothing broken, I hope?

Luckily not. Though I might easily have sprained something...

YEOW!

It's a bad sprain... and you've pulled the ligaments.

?

Tomorrow I'll put it in plaster...

In plaster!!... A sprained ankle?!... But doctor, I'm leaving today for Italy.

Out of the question. Absolute rest with the foot in plaster for a fortnight. Think yourself fortunate you didn't break a leg.

And my advice to you is, get that step repaired. Someone else might not have your good luck... Goodbye.

Goodbye, doctor.

Luck? If that's luck, give me disaster!!

CUCKOO

!

Ah, dear Captain Fatstock!... How too divine to see you again!

How... how did you get in?

Misericordia! What has happened to you?

A sprain! But... how did you get in?

Just as we arrived, dear Tintin was showing someone out. So we didn't need to ring.

"We"? There can't be more than one of you!

But of course! Irma, my maid, always travels with me...

...and so does my accompanist, Igor Wagner, who obvious-ly has to... ha! ha!ha ...accompany me!

8

Excuse me, signora, may I introduce our old friend Professor Calculus.

How enchanting, how absolutely thrilling to meet you: the man who makes all those daring ascents in balloons!

POP

!

I am deeply honoured, signora. What a rare pleasure for me to meet so great an artist... an artist of such charm, such distinction, such...

Professor, you make me blush!

I sincerely hope so, signora. Tintin has often spoken of your pictures...the delicacy of the drawing in perfect harmony with the boldness of the colour. And your portraits, I know, always display an amazing likeness.

Nestor, please show the signora to her room.

Yes, sir.

How kind... But first...er... Irma, where is the...er...the little something for dear Captain Drydock?

!

In the taxi, madame. I'll fetch it.

I thought... I thought that an old sailorman like yourself must feel very lonely in his little boat... Il povero capitano!

That's very kind of you, but...

I knew you'd adore...

Here, Madame.

?

...this pretty polly to be your constant companion.

?!?

I... What a... surprise!... What a delightful surprise!... Nothing could have given me...er... greater pleasure.

Aha! I knew it!

Here, Irma, put him on his perch.

Yes, madame.

I can't stand animals who talk!

They've unloaded the luggage. This is where she's staying... To work, Gino!

He's called Iago, a compliment to dear Signor Verdi... He's so affectionate... We love nice Captain Hopscotch already, don't we?

Stroke him, Captain, don't be afraid; he wouldn't hurt a fly.

KILIKILIKILIKILI!

How sweet!...He's taken to you already ...Ah, animals have an unfailing instinct: they immediately attach themselves to those they love.

You think so?

CRO!

YEOWWW!

Billions of bilious blue blistering barbecued barnacles!... Cannibal! ...Bashi-bazouk!... Vampire!

Hello-o-o! I can hear you!

Please, Captain Stopcock! Such language! ...Poor pollikins might learn it!...Show me your hand.

CRO!

Now, now... our finger is just a teeny-weeny bit sore... Irmaaa!...The first aid things, please!

Here is the case, madame...and... this...

Of course, I forgot! Dear Tintin, this is just a little gift from me to you.

?

There we are...A pretty little butterfly to comfort the poor sailorman.

The Jewel Song!

I'm very grateful, signora. It was very kind of you to think of me.

Not at all, not at all! I thought it would remind you of our first meeting in Syldavia. Do you remember?

Shall I ever forget it! Of course, that was the first time I heard you sing the Jewel Song from "Faust".

Ah, yes, the Jewel Song ...

MERCY!... MY JEWELS!

Here, madame; I've got your jewel-case.

Oh, so you have. I can breathe again!

Now, my man, if you'd be kind enough to show me to my room ...

As the signora wishes.

Oh, I almost forgot... The reporters will probably run me to earth here. May I ask my brave sailor to protect me?... Not a single interview, no publicity, no photographs... nothing! I came here incognito; you must help me to escape.

Of course!

May I point out to the signora that the fourth step is broken.

Yes, yes, I see.

The signora's room.

Ravishing!

What delightful old furniture! ...and a four-poster bed. It's... er... Henry the Tenth, is it not?

Charles the First, signora.

Precisely what I meant, of course.

DONG

If the signora will excuse me: the door-bell.

You may go.

Fiddle! What is it now?

Oh dear!...The step!

Well done, Nestor, ... always keep your head!

!

I'll put the telephone here, Captain, where you can reach it.

Thanks, Tintin, that's very kind.

Oh sir!... In the drive...a whole horde of gipsies!...They say you told them to come, sir... you invited them to camp in the grounds.

That's right, Nestor. Show them into the big meadow, down by the stream.

But sir!... If I may make so bold, sir... Gipsies, sir... Nothing but a bunch of thieving rogues...They'll only make trouble for you, sir.

Trouble!!

How can I be in worse trouble? ...Go and see to them, Nestor...

But...I...er...Very good, sir.

Would you like me to go, Captain? Nestor has so much to do in the house already.

Thanks.

Inviting gipsies to stay!

He's mad...He's absolutely mad!...He'll come a cropper one of these days!...

THUMP

Blistering barnacles, that step! Why can't people look where they're going!

RRRING

Hello...Yes, Haddock here... Who's that?...The police! ... What?!?

Ah, Captain: my men report that some gipsies who were camping by the main road have moved ...It seems you invited them to pitch camp on your land ...Is that so?

Quite correct, Inspector. I think it's intolerable! Those wretched creatures forbidden to camp except on a rubbish dump! And as I have a meadow...

Hello-o-o! I can hear you!

Hello?...What?...You can hear me?...Well, I can hear you. And since we can hear each other, let me say I quite understand your action, Captain. It's most generous... I beg your pardon ...Did you say shut up?

No...not you!...I'm talking to this pestilential parakeet! Will you shut up, you ...

Hello-o-o! I can hear you!

Ah, I see. You're still addressing your parrot... Now, about those gipsies. Of course, you're free to do as you like. But I should warn you: you'll only have yourself to thank when they make trouble for you.

Trouble!...Ha! ha! First I'm bitten by a little wildcat, then by a parrot!...I sprain an ankle... Castafiore descends on me with Irma and that budding Beethoven... And they talk about trouble!... Ha! ha! ha! ha!...

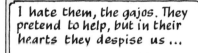

Meanwhile ...

Mission completed: all settled in.

I hate them, the gajos. They pretend to help, but in their hearts they despise us ...

Not these, Mike, not these.

GRRR! WOOAH! WOOAH! GRRR!

Hello, what's up? Snowy's got wind of something.

WOOAH! WOOAH! GRRR! GRRR!

Snowy!... Here, Snowy!

?

WOOAH! WOOAH!

Hey, who are you?... Stop!

WOOAH! WOOAH!

The gap!...They're going through the gap in the wall!

Wooah!

A car!

Wooah!

VROOMM

!

What's the meaning of that? ...And what shall I do?... Tell the Captain?...No, he's got enough on his plate already.

RRRING

Hello?...Hello?... Can you hear me?

?

Rrrring Rrrring Rrrring

KRRTCHMURTZ !

Mercy, my jewels!

I'll lock my jewels in this drawer, Irma...

...and I'll hide the key to the drawer in this vase, over here. Try to remember, girl.

Yes, madame.

That's that, Captain. Our gipsy friends are installed. They're delighted with their new camp.

Good. I'm very glad.

Hello-o-o-o! I can hear you!

That parrot!...It'll drive me crazy!...Anyway, it's nearly bedtime. Then at least I'll be free of it for the night!
...

Nuts!

That night...

AH! MY BEAUTY

E-E-EEK!

!

O Dio!... Dio mio!...

What's happened?

There... in my room... at the window... a monster!

A monster?

There's nothing here, signora. Absolutely nothing.

But I did; I saw a monster, I tell you... A ghost or something... It was horrible... I heard a long, mournful cry, and I saw two eyes shining like diam...

MERCY! MY JEWELS! IRMAAA! MY JEWELS?!

No, no, madame: they are quite safe.

TUWIT – TUWOO

O Dio! That voice!

The cry of the monster!... Listen!

That?... But that's only a bird: just a poor old night-owl!

Are you sure? And the footsteps on the ceiling?

On the ceiling?

Yes, I heard someone walking about upstairs... It was a man, I'm certain.

Impossible, signora. It's only the attic above, and no one lives up there.

But I assure you...

Don't be afraid, signora. Go back to sleep... and close your window; then you won't need to worry.

The next morning...

I might just have a look under Signora Castafiore's window.

That's the one...

Well, well, well...

15

Footprints!...Right under the window!... Was she telling the truth, then?

The ivy?

No. It would never support a man's weight...A child, maybe?...But then there'd be traces of the climb...Anyway, the footprints are those of an adult...

...But whose? That's the problem...Someone from the house?...One of the two strangers I chased yesterday? ...A gipsy?

Here, Snowy. We'll take a walk down by the encampment.

If there are any footprints, they'll show up in the mud. So let's go where they water their horses.

No, none like those we saw in the flowerbed.

SPLASH

?!

WOOAH! WOOAH!

Come on, Snowy. We shan't find our humorous friend by staying here...

There he goes. Ha! ha! He didn't wait for a second round, the little brat. I don't like the way he's always snooping around.

So, that's who it was...that gipsy...he threw the stone. But why?

We don't seem to be much further on ...Come on Snowy, ...home.

That's the doctor leaving: he'll have put the Captain's foot in plaster. But there's another car...Who does that belong to?

Let's see . . .

Why, it's Mr. Wagg. Hello!

Hello-o-o! I can hear you!

Hi there, boyo!

I was just passing: a client to see near here for the old Rock Bottom Insurance. So I said to myself: "Jolyon," I said, "now's your chance to say howdy to the ancient mariner". And look what I find: the old humbug's fallen downstairs!

What a scream! Anyway, a bit of luck I popped in. A proper godsend, that's me. This lady was just telling me about last night's caper. And what does Jolyon Wagg discover? . . . Hold on to your hats . . .

Her jewels, her famous jewels, aren't even insured! What about that? A proper carry-on, eh?

Worth thousands and thousands . . . She's got one little sparkler, an emerald . . . Given to her out East by some character . . . Marjorie something or other . . .

Maharajah . . . The Maharajah of Gopal.

That's the chap. And that little tit-bit alone is worth a fortune. Crazy what you get for a song, eh? Beats me. Not that I've got anything against music, but between you and me, I prefer a dollop of wallop any day.

Not a single jewel covered. So I said: "Lady, you give me a list of your knick-knacks, and Jolyon Wagg will insure the whole shoot!" . . .

I'll consider it, Mr. Bag.

Fiddlesticks! . . . It's all fixed . . . I'll be back in a day or two with a policy. Cheerio for now, Duchess. Pleased to meet you!

. . . And if I were you, Lord Nelson, I'd get that step fixed.

It had occurred to me! I'm waiting for the builder.

DONG

That's probably him now at the door.

This Halibut's house?

No, Haddock's. Why?

REMOVALS
BOUNCE Bros

V12277-7

We've brought the piano.

The piano?

Piano??

Piano???

Oh, yes, the piano!... It's mine. I hired a piano, to practise with Mr. Wagner. I do hope you don't mind...

Of course not, I'm over-joyed.

You sweet old thing!... In that case they can put it in here, so we can cheer you up.

I... er... thank you; but the maritime gallery would be better for you.

Admirable!... Mr. Wagner, just see to it, will you?

Certainly, signora.

Thundering typhoons, she'll have a jukebox next!

Is that piano for you?

Yes, it is.

Excuse me, your shoe-lace is undone.

Why, so it is.

!

RRRRING

Drat that parrot!

RRRING

Hello, yes... Speaking ..."Paris-Flash International"? I beg your pardon?... What? An interview?... I... er... I'm very flattered... Gladly ...

I can hear you!

Oh! An interview with Signora Castafiore!... I... er... I'm very sorry, but Signora Castafiore has asked me to say...

Allow me... "Paris-Flash"? ...Hello-o-o! ... I can hear you!

?

Yes, this is me... Of course I'm me... An interview?... Naturally... with pleasure. Whenever you like... Very well. I shall look forward to tomorrow... Ciao!

Those footprints... they were made by the little pianist... Very odd ...

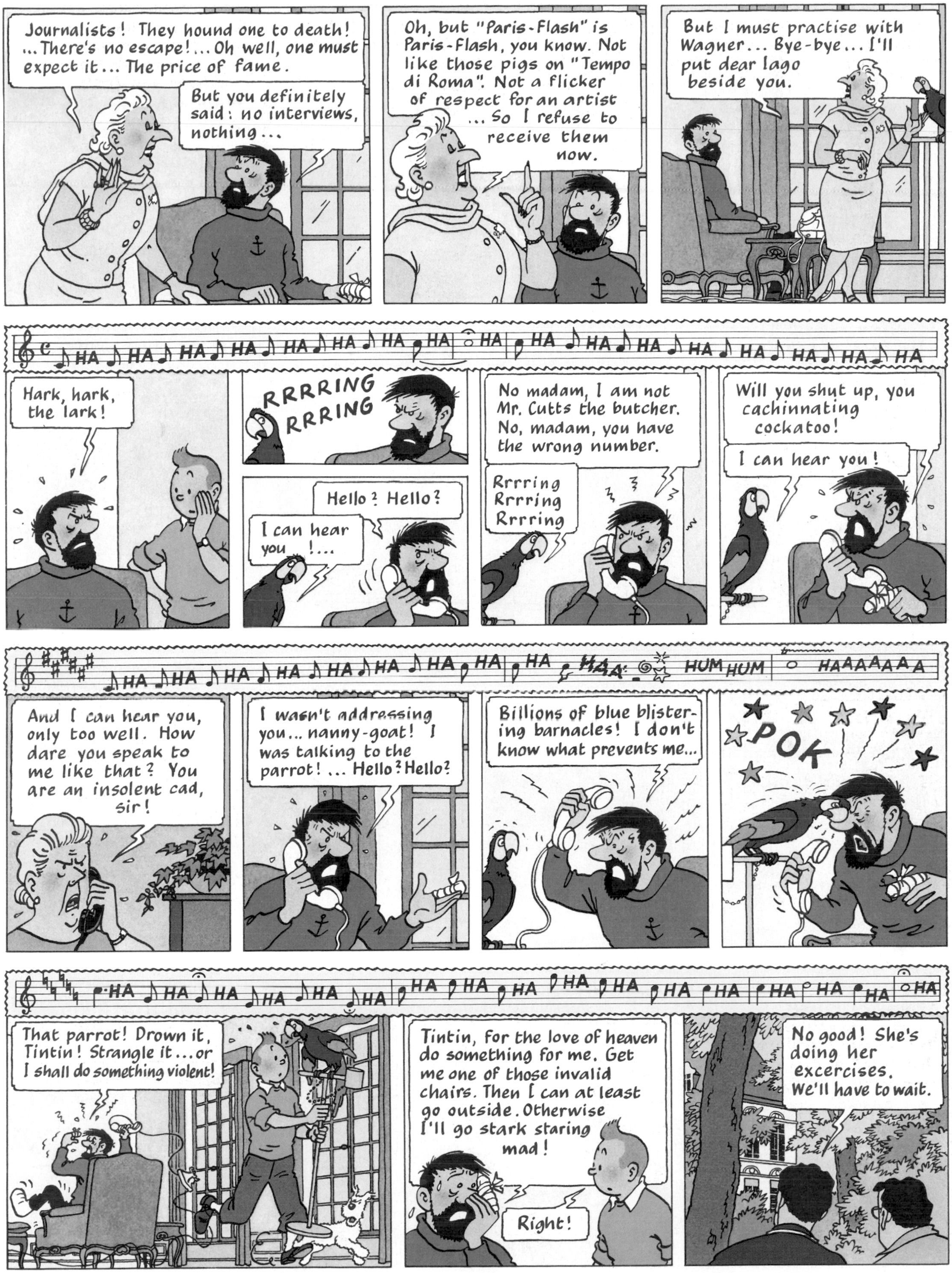
Journalists! They hound one to death! ... There's no escape! ... Oh well, one must expect it... The price of fame.
But you definitely said: no interviews, nothing...
Oh, but "Paris-Flash" is Paris-Flash, you know. Not like those pigs on "Tempo di Roma". Not a flicker of respect for an artist ... So I refuse to receive them now.
But I must practise with Wagner... Bye-bye... I'll put dear Iago beside you.
HA HA HA HA HA HA HA HA HA HA HA HA HA HA HA HA HA HA HA HA
Hark, hark, the lark!
RRRRING RRRING
Hello? Hello?
I can hear you!...
No madam, I am not Mr. Cutts the butcher. No, madam, you have the wrong number.
Rrrring Rrrring Rrrring
Will you shut up, you cachinnating cockatoo!
I can hear you!
HA HA HA HA HA HA HA HA HA HA HAA HUM HUM HAAAAAAA
And I can hear you, only too well. How dare you speak to me like that? You are an insolent cad, sir!
I wasn't addressing you... nanny-goat! I was talking to the parrot! ... Hello? Hello?
Billions of blue blistering barnacles! I don't know what prevents me...
POK
HA HA HA HA HA HA HA HA HA HA HA HA HA HA HA HA HA HA
That parrot! Drown it, Tintin! Strangle it... or I shall do something violent!
Tintin, for the love of heaven do something for me. Get me one of those invalid chairs. Then I can at least go outside. Otherwise I'll go stark staring mad!
Right!
No good! She's doing her excercises. We'll have to wait.

The next morning...

Yes, I know... I couldn't help it. I had to finish a tombstone: it was urgent. What? Yours is urgent too: yes, I know... Look, I'll be there first thing tomorrow morning... Yes, without fail.

If he's not here tomorrow I'll get someone else, and that's flat.

Captain! Captain!

Here's your new racing car.

♪HA ♪HA ♪HA

Hooray! I'm free!

Wooah! Wooah!

♪HA ♪HA ♪HA ♪HA ♪HA ♪HA

Peace at last... And there's old Cuthbert, pruning his roses...

Meanwhile...

Ah, Paris-Flash! Come in gentlemen. I will inform the signora.

Hello, Cuthbert. Working already this morning?

Very well, thank you. And you?... How's the foot?

Oh, not so bad!... Anyway, I might have broken my leg... Then I really should have looked a fool.

Cool? In the shade, perhaps, but in the sun it's really quite hot.

Great news, Captain - but this is strictly between ourselves - I have succeeded in raising a completely new variety of rose.

Well done! Splendid!... Better than building rockets and chasing off into the blue.

No, no, white!... But such a white! ... Pearly, sparkling, immaculate! ... And the shape - perfect!... And what perfume - exquisite!

Well, Professor, I congratulate you.

OW!

And the name? Aha! You will never guess...

What was that? Who shouted?

I've had an idea - I think I may say an inspiration.

Hi!... Stop, who-ever you are!

Idiot! Did you have to put your your great feet into a wasps' nest?

As I told you, the rose I have created is white. Now, what is white in Italian?

Bianca, of course... Bianca! You follow me?

Bianca! Bianca!... Who were those ectoplasms, bolting like rabbits? That's what interests me!

Yes, Bianca, like our delightful guest. This rose shall be called "Bianca Castafiore". A charming compliment, don't you think?

The scoundrels! I'll bet they were up to no good!

But the world must wait... You mustn't breathe a word, I implore you. It must be a complete surprise.

What?... Which?... A surprise?... For whom?

That's agreed, isn't it?... I can count on you... This is strictly between ourselves.

Strangers in the park... What's it all about?

Hello, who's that on the seat? Oh, it's...

IRMAAA!

?

IRMAAA!

Yes, madame.

Where are you, Irma?

Here madame. I'm coming.

Take cover!

Have you seen Captain Hammock? I simply must find him.

!

If you see him, tell him we've finished. These gentlemen from "Paris-Flash" have concluded their interview and would so like to meet him.

Yes, madame.

Disaster! They're coming this way. I'm caught like a rat in a trap!

You know, he's just a dear old sea-dog, a bit crusty at first, but...

...beneath a rough exterior he hides the simple heart of a big, lovable child.

There he is, asleep, and in the shade, too.

Zzzz... Zzzz...

Captain Paddock! Oh, you naughty man, look at you, asleep in the shade! You'll catch your death of cold!

What?...Oh, I must have been asleep.

Look, I've brought your coat. It's chilly out here...Now, now, now!

But I'm not cold!

I see I must scold you for something else, too... That jersey, it really won't do on a man of your age!

But ...

It's like your hair!... When will you learn to do it properly, and stop looking like a scruffy little schoolboy?

But ...

Let me introduce Christopher Willoughby-Drupe and Marco Rizotto of "Paris-Flash".

Hello!

'Morning.

Well, gentlemen, now that you've all met, I will release you. Roam about in the grounds as you please. Captain Hassock and I will expect you to lunch.

Now, my dear, let us have a little chat.

Well, what do you make of it?

The same as you, chum! This is a sensation ... But we must be sure...

True or not, Marco my boy, it'll sell!

I can just see the cover!

Look, a gardener. Come on, we'll try to pump him.

O.K.!

But...it isn't the gardener... it's Professor Calculus, who went to the moon with Tintin. He should be in the know.

Let's go!

Good morning, Professor. May we introduce ourselves: Christopher Willoughby-Drupe and Marco Rizotto of "Paris-Flash". Here's our card.

From the Yard?

Reporters!...So that's it! The Captain had to tell someone. He's already tattled to the papers about my new rose, the old gossip!

Tell me, Professor, off the record, isn't there something in the wind between La Castafiore and Captain Haddock?... Plans for a wedding?... Am I right?

It was the Captain who told you, wasn't it?

Well... yes and no... You know how it is... we reporters ...flair, you understand ... So it's true?

Great sunspots! And he promised to say nothing! It was to have been a surprise...

I quite understand ...How soon will it be?

It all depends on the weather ... But it could happen any day now.

Aha! So it's imminent, then! And... how long has this been fixed? Can you give any little snippets about them ...How they first met, for example?

Precisely!... It was two years ago ...

...at the Chelsea Flower Show. But ssh! Here she comes ... Signora Bianca, with the Captain. Not a word about this!

Right!

Er... the Professor was telling us...er...about his roses. How magnificent they are!

Exquisite. I was just saying so to Captain Havoc.

Meanwhile . . .

Got that? Sugarplum... Oriana ...Semiramis...

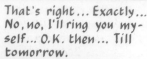

That's right... Exactly... No, no, I'll ring you myself... O.K. then... Till tomorrow.

Oh, how I adore flowers! They bring them in armfuls, but I never get tired of them!

Dear lady, allow me to offer you this modest "Crimson Glory"... until... er... something better comes along... Ha! ha!

Oh, Professor!

MMMM! What a sweet scent!

Smell, Captain!... Inhale the fragrance... Exquisite, isn't it?

YEOW!

Billions of blistering barnacles! I've been stung by a bee!

My poor boy, how did you manage to do that? And what a terrible fuss! You frightened me to death! Wait, I'll help you. First remove the sting... There! Then apply crushed rose petals to the spot.

Th-e-re! Better already, aren't we?

Now, my friends, I'll leave you. I must change for lunch... Ciao!

Trala laaa ♪ ♫ ♪

You're looking for Captain Maggot, I'm sure. You'll find him in the rose garden. The poor darling, he's been stung on the nose by a bee.

Oh!

A bee-sting on the nose... Poor Captain; that could be horribly painful.

E-E-EEK! MY NECKLACE!

24

IRMA-A-A! IRMA-A-A!

Yes, madame.

Oh, it's you!... Something frightful has happened: I've just broken my neck-lace!

Don't worry, signora. I'm sure we'll find all the beads.

There you are at last! I've been calling you for hours. You should have been here to pick up my necklace.

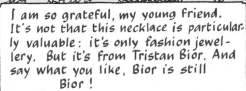

I am so grateful, my young friend. It's not that this necklace is particularly valuable: it's only fashion jewellery. But it's from Tristan Bior. And say what you like, Bior is still Bior!

Er... obviously!

Now let's see about the Captain's nose.

Don't think I'm angry with you, Captain, but why did you tell them about my rose?

What? Your rose?

Your rose! Will you shut up about your rose! Blistering barnacles, if I hadn't had one shoved in my face, I shouldn't have a nose like an overgrown strawberry!

Oh no, white!

Excuse me, madame, have you seen my embroidery scissors... you know, the little gold ones...

Why should I have seen them, girl? It's not my job to look after your things.

I didn't say that, madame ... It's strange, I had them earlier, when you called me the first time; when I returned to my seat I couldn't find them.

Well, have a good look, my child... No one's going to steal a pair of scissors, are they?

No, madame.

Meanwhile...

Little scissors made of gold... Aren't they pretty, Uncle Mike?

Very nice!

Hello, is that Mr. Bolt?... Oh, I'm speaking to Mrs. Bolt...

Yes... oh, the gentleman from the Hall... Er... no, he's been gone since first thing this morning... Oh? He promised to come to you?... I'm afraid I don't know... I'll tell him, sir... Yes, without fail, sir...

Thundering typhoons! If he doesn't come tomorrow I'll get someone else...

RRRING

?

Hello, is that you, old shipmate?...This is Jolyon... Congratulations! ...You old humbug, you certainly had your old pal fooled! ...

Had you fooled? Me?...I don't understand... What do you mean?

Ha! ha! ha! Still keeping your trap shut, eh? ... That's O.K. by me!... Keep your hair on. I just wanted to be first to congratulate you.

But...

And don't let your Castafiore do anything about that insurance: I've got to go off on the road for a while, but I haven't forgotten it...I'll be back one of these days... Well, so long, old horse. And once again: all the best!
= CLICK =

I...

Congratulations? What's that gas-bag on about now?

Oh well, forget it. I'll have a quiet pipe, and read the papers.

DONG

Now what is it?

A telegram for you, sir.

A telegram?

Billions of blistering barnacles! What does this mean?

Read that and tell me if it conveys anything to you. And that idiot Wagg has just rung up to congratulate me.

Oh?

Heartiest congratulations. Captain Chester...

Doesn't make sense, does it?

WHAT?

BROL

SCOOP!

PARISH FLASH INTERNATIONAL

MILANESE NIGHTINGALE BIANCA CASTAFIORE WILL MARRY OLD SEA LION

At the Chelsea Flower Show, famed the world over for its exotic blooms, Bianca Castafiore met her future husband, retired Admiral Hammock. Our reporters have been to Marlinspike Hall, to bring you these intimate glimpses of two happy people.

MY LOVE IS LIKE A RED, RED ROSE...

He opens his heart to the parrot she gave him.

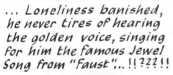

... Loneliness banished, he never tires of hearing the golden voice, singing for him the famous Jewel Song from "Faust"...!!???!!

Blistering barnacles! Wait till I get my hands on the miserable molecule of mildew who dreamed up this balderdash!

Hello-o-o! I can hear you!

CRO!

BROL

Buon giorno, Tintin! Buon giorno, Captain Bootblack!

!" ?"

Have you seen the marvellous article about me in "Paris-Flash"?

Yes, I have seen it, madam!... You call it marvellous?...Announcing our marriage!

Oh, yes, priceless, isn't it?

But it doesn't mean a thing. The newspapers have already engaged me to the Maharajah of Gopal, to Baron Halmaszout, the Lord Chamberlain of Syldavia, to Colonel Sponsz, to the Marquis di Gorgonzola, and goodness knows who. So you see, I'm quite used to it...

Well I'm not, madam, and I...

RRRING

HELLO!

This is Thompson and Thomson, with a 'p' and without... Our west bishes...er...our wet dishes... I mean, many congratulations, Captain. We've just seen "Paris-Flash".

KOUA KOUAKOUIN KOUIN-KOUIN KOUA KOUIN KOUA... BANG!

Nitwitted ninepins!

How very odd: not a word about my rose.

But... but... oh, goodness! ... Goodness gracious! ... Goodness gracious me!

My dear friend!... My dear old friend! Most hearty congratulations!... How happy I am to hear the news! But why didn't you tell me before?

A few telegrams, sir. And may I be allowed, sir, to offer my most respectful felicitations.

Good wishes, Cutts the butcher... Congratulations, Mr and Mrs Bolt... Sincere greetings, Doctor Patella... My most delighted good wishes, Oliveira da Figueira...

Hello? ...Yes...yes ...Supavision... One moment, please...

It's a television company, sir... They want...

Now television!!

Oh no! Leave me alone! I refuse to behave like a performing seal in front of a camera!

But sir...

There's no but about it... I've had enough of reporters!... Tell them I'm out!

But sir, it's Signora Castafiore they wish to speak to.

To me? But my good man, why didn't you say so before?

Hello-o-o!...Yes, I can hear you!... Supavision?...Yes... I'd adore to... When?... Tomorrow... Lovely... yes... I shall look forward to seeing you!

What a bore they are!... But what can one do?... They'll be here tomorrow afternoon.

Someone here must have given all this to the reporters. I wonder who it was?

Oh, what a charming idea! An aubade!

Your ladyship, Captain sir...

Ssh!

But...

On behalf of the Marlinspike Prize Band Supporters' Club I have the honour to present to you with due deference the respectful congratulations of all our members on this felicitous event, which has brought...

... a light to every throat and a lump in every eye...

You must offer them champagne...

What?...Champagne? ...Never!

Several glasses later...

The following afternoon...

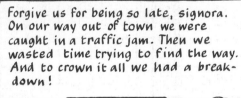

Forgive us for being so late, signora. On our way out of town we were caught in a traffic jam. Then we wasted time trying to find the way. And to crown it all we had a breakdown!

Did you? How priceless!

Thundering typhoons! This is a full-scale invasion!

Oh, sorry!

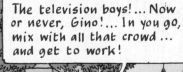

The television boys!... Now or never, Gino!... In you go, mix with all that crowd... and get to work!

I'll wait in the car just down the road... O.K.?

O.K. I'll take my gear and chance it...

I'm inside, anyway...

With that flood you can light the ceiling.

I'd better explain... It's a telerecording and we're also putting it on film.

Ah, I see... Perhaps we can talk more easily sitting down.

Right... I shall appear in the first sequence and say a few words of introduction. Then I put the first question, and the cameras focus on you. From then on I shall only be heard 'off'.

Ah!

At the end of that sequence I shall ask if you'll be kind enough to sing... something specially for the viewers.

Naturally, with pleasure.

Thank you. For the second sequence, you cross slowly to the piano, where your accompanist will be waiting, and you sing... What will you sing, signora?

I...er...well... what about the Jewel Song from "Faust", for instance?

Excellent...Afterwards, I close the interview with a few words of thanks.

Just so!

We're ready, Andy...what about you?

All O.K. I'd just like to do a voice test, and we're all set.

Take up the mike, Jim. It's in the picture...

Don't mind me, lady. This is only a light meter.

Good...How's that for balance? ... Silence!...Sound on!

Vision on!

Good evening, viewers. Tonight is rather a special occasion. We are visiting the eminent singer, Bianca Castafiore... All right like that?

So far everything's going like clockwork!

O.K. for sound!

Good. Now, signora, just a few words from you, please.

Er... My turn now? ... Just a few words? ... Well... I... I... I'm happy... so very... happy... Well, I don't really know how to put it... Ah! ha! ha!

O.K. for sound!

Right. Stand by! Silence now, boys and girls!

Sound on!

Vision on!

O.K ...Let's roll!

CLACK

Good evening, viewers. Tonight is a very special occasion. We are visiting the eminent singer, Bianca Castafiore, of La Scala, Milan, so aptly called "the Milanese nightingale"...

Tell me, signora... is it indiscreet to ask the reason for your presence at Marlinspike?

Well, my last tour of the West Indies (a triumph, by the way) was so exhausting ... and as I knew that Captain Balzac and his friends ...

... would welcome me with open arms, I had no hesitation in inviting my-self to stay.

Why, you've installed tele-vision! ... Three sets at once!! ... And you never even told me ?!?

Ssh!

Oh! look ... that's... that's Sig-nora Castafiore!... Yes, I assure you it is!... Good gracious! Someone must tell her at once!

She must see it, the dear lady. She simply must!

Professor! Professor!! Don't go in there. They're shooting!

E-E-EEK!

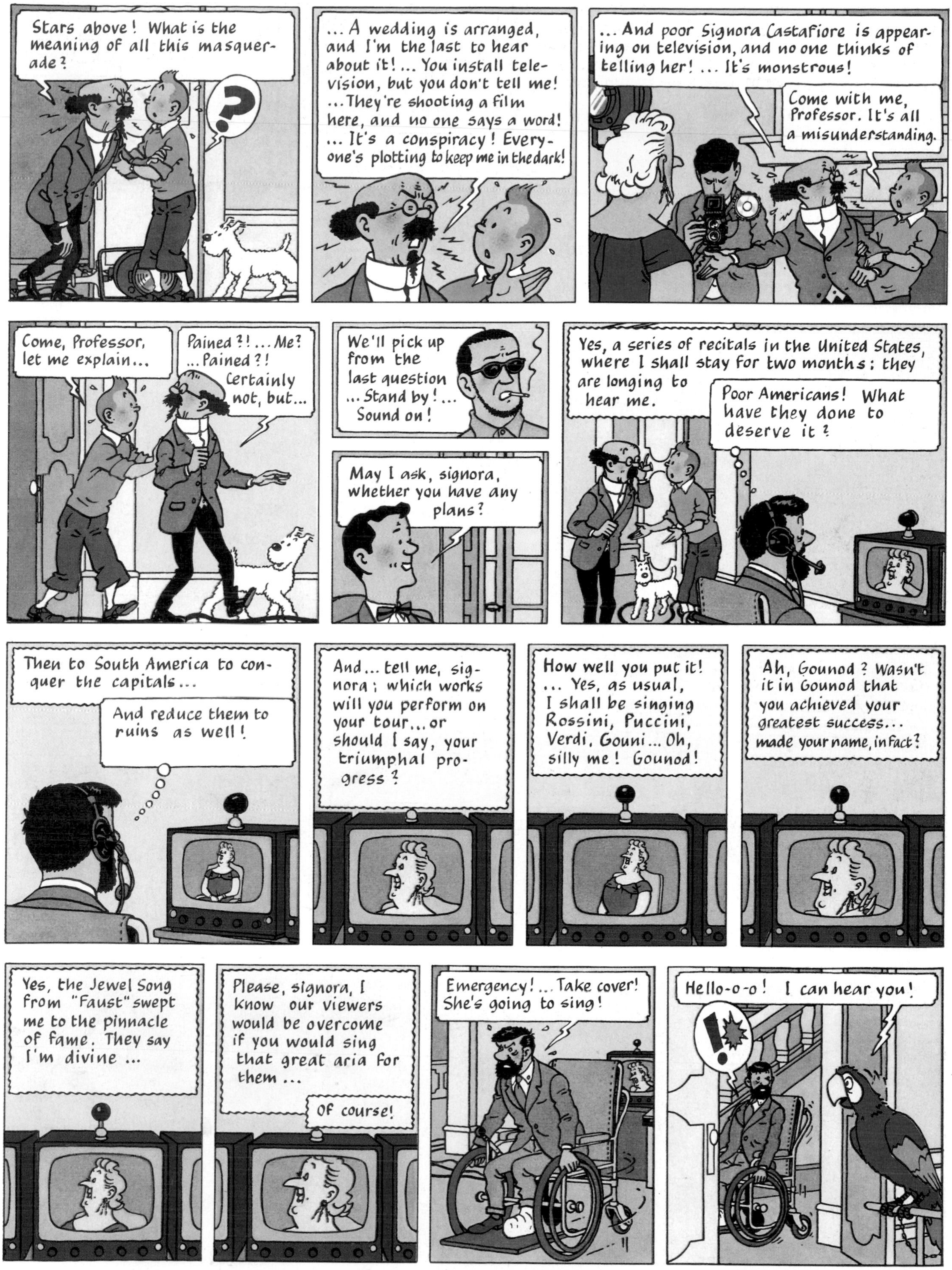
Stars above! What is the meaning of all this masquerade?
... A wedding is arranged, and I'm the last to hear about it! ... You install television, but you don't tell me! ... They're shooting a film here, and no one says a word! ... It's a conspiracy! Everyone's plotting to keep me in the dark!
... And poor Signora Castafiore is appearing on television, and no one thinks of telling her! ... It's monstrous!
Come with me, Professor. It's all a misunderstanding.
Come, Professor, let me explain...
Pained?! ... Me? ... Pained?! Certainly not, but...
We'll pick up from the last question ... Stand by! ... Sound on!
May I ask, signora, whether you have any plans?
Yes, a series of recitals in the United States, where I shall stay for two months: they are longing to hear me.
Poor Americans! What have they done to deserve it?
Then to South America to conquer the capitals...
And reduce them to ruins as well!
And... tell me, signora; which works will you perform on your tour... or should I say, your triumphal progress?
How well you put it! ... Yes, as usual, I shall be singing Rossini, Puccini, Verdi, Gouni... Oh, silly me! Gounod!
Ah, Gounod? Wasn't it in Gounod that you achieved your greatest success... made your name, in fact?
Yes, the Jewel Song from "Faust" swept me to the pinnacle of fame. They say I'm divine ...
Please, signora, I know our viewers would be overcome if you would sing that great aria for them ...
Of course!
Emergency! ... Take cover! She's going to sing!
Hello-o-o! I can hear you!

Come on, let's press on. It's getting late.

Vision on!

Stand by! ...Sound on!

AAAAH! ♩ My beauty...

...past compare these jewels bright I wear

AAAH! My beauty

In you go!

I CAN HEAR YOU!

Sacrilege! Who dares to interrupt?

Cut!

Madamina!...It's Iago; he's escaped from his perch!

How clever animals are! And what a true instinct they have for art! Look at darling Iago; obviously he couldn't resist my voice!...But come, my pet, I must take you back. Excuse me, I won't be a moment.

Oh, there you are, Captain Bedsock. Just imagine, Iago got free from his perch all by himself, just to come and hear me!

Hmm!... Amazing!

Meanwhile...

Quick as you can, now... All ready? ...Quiet studio please!

Tell me, ♪ was I ever Marga ...

... RITA...?!

Damn! A blackout!

This is the last straw!

The fuses, I expect...

Anyone got a match?

☆ HELP!

MERCY! MY JEWELS!

Mind the cables!

34

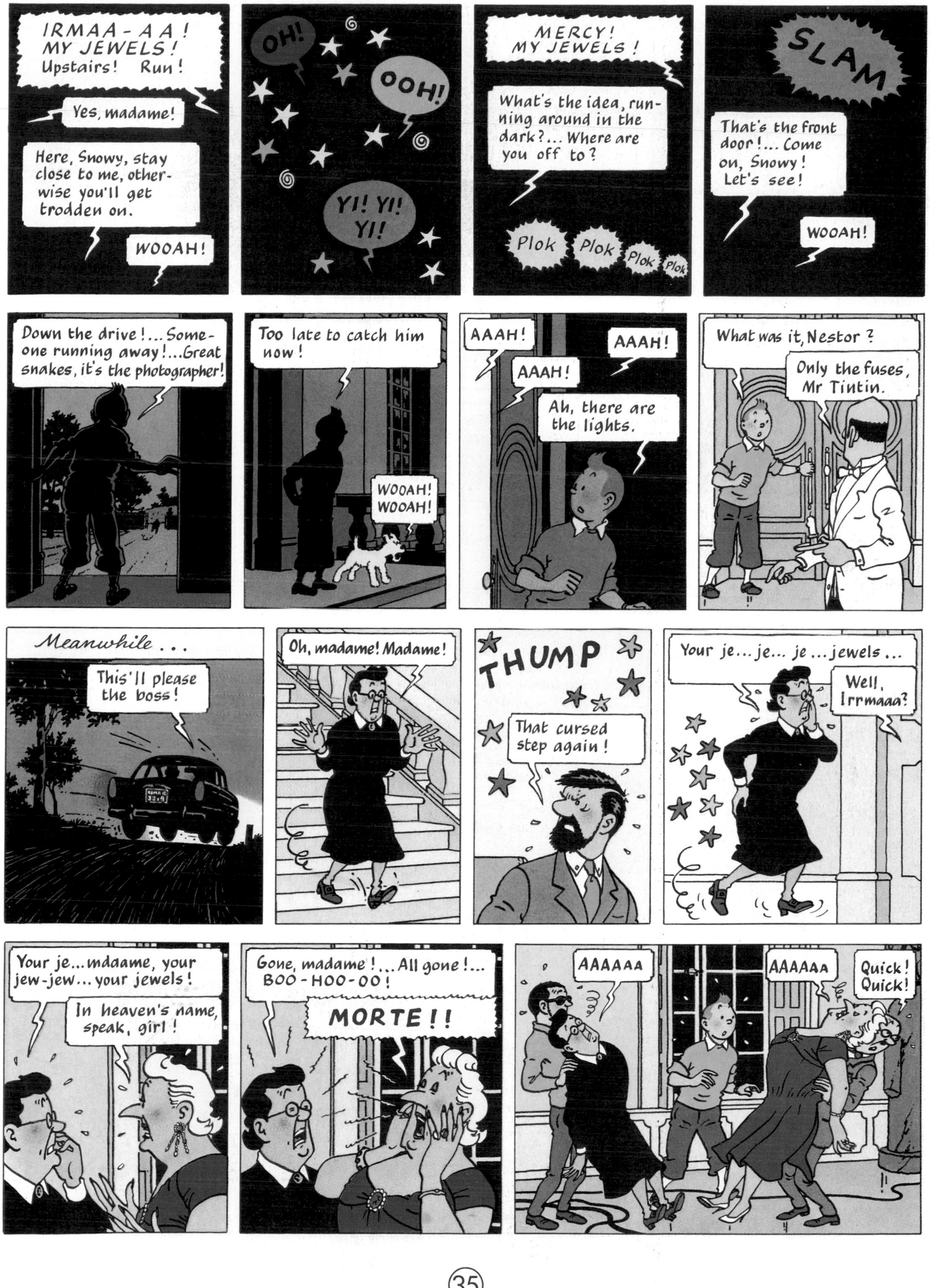
IRMAA-AA! MY JEWELS! Upstairs! Run!
Yes, madame!
Here, Snowy, stay close to me, otherwise you'll get trodden on.
WOOAH!
OH!
OOH!
YI! YI! YI!
MERCY! MY JEWELS!
What's the idea, running around in the dark?... Where are you off to?
Plok Plok Plok Plok
SLAM
That's the front door!... Come on, Snowy! Let's see!
WOOAH!
Down the drive!... Someone running away!... Great snakes, it's the photographer!
Too late to catch him now!
WOOAH! WOOAH!
AAAH!
AAAH!
AAAH!
Ah, there are the lights.
What was it, Nestor?
Only the fuses, Mr Tintin.
Meanwhile ...
This'll please the boss!
Oh, madame! Madame!
THUMP
That cursed step again!
Your je... je... je... jewels...
Well, Irrmaaa?
Your je... mdaame, your jew-jew... your jewels!
In heaven's name, speak, girl!
Gone, madame!... All gone!... BOO-HOO-OO!
MORTE!!
AAAAAA
AAAAAA
Quick! Quick!

AAAAAA

?

Over there! on the sofa!

Hey!... Here's another out cold!

We must ring the police at once.

Smelling salts... She needs smelling salts!

A fine carry-on!

I knew it would happen!... Boo-hoo-hoo!... I knew it would!

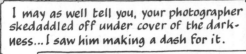

I may as well tell you, your photographer skedaddled off under cover of the darkness... I saw him making a dash for it.

Our photographer?... Who?... The photographer who was here just now? He was nothing to do with us.

But I thought he belonged to your outfit.

And I thought he was a private photographer engaged by Signora Castafiore.

Hello?... Marlinspike police?... This is Captain...what?

I said: wrong number, sir. This is Cutts the butcher... Not at all sir...

Hello?... Marlinspike police?... Oh, good... This is Captain Haddock.

Good evening, Inspector... Can you send someone along here at once?... There's been a serious robbery... What?!... A stroke of luck?!

What?... Who?... No?!... They were with you? Good heavens! ... On their way? They'll be here any minute now?... But what were they doing... Yes... I see... All right, I'll wait till they arrive ... Goodbye, Inspector.

Blistering barnacles, what were those two ostrogoths doing at Marlinspike police station?

So the photographer did it... That's odd... very odd indeed!

I know that look: it means trouble!

Oh, there you are, Tintin... We have visitors coming; you'll never guess who!

Oh?...

BOANG GLING ZZING BING-GLING DING CLING

?

!?

Hello-o-o! I can hear you!

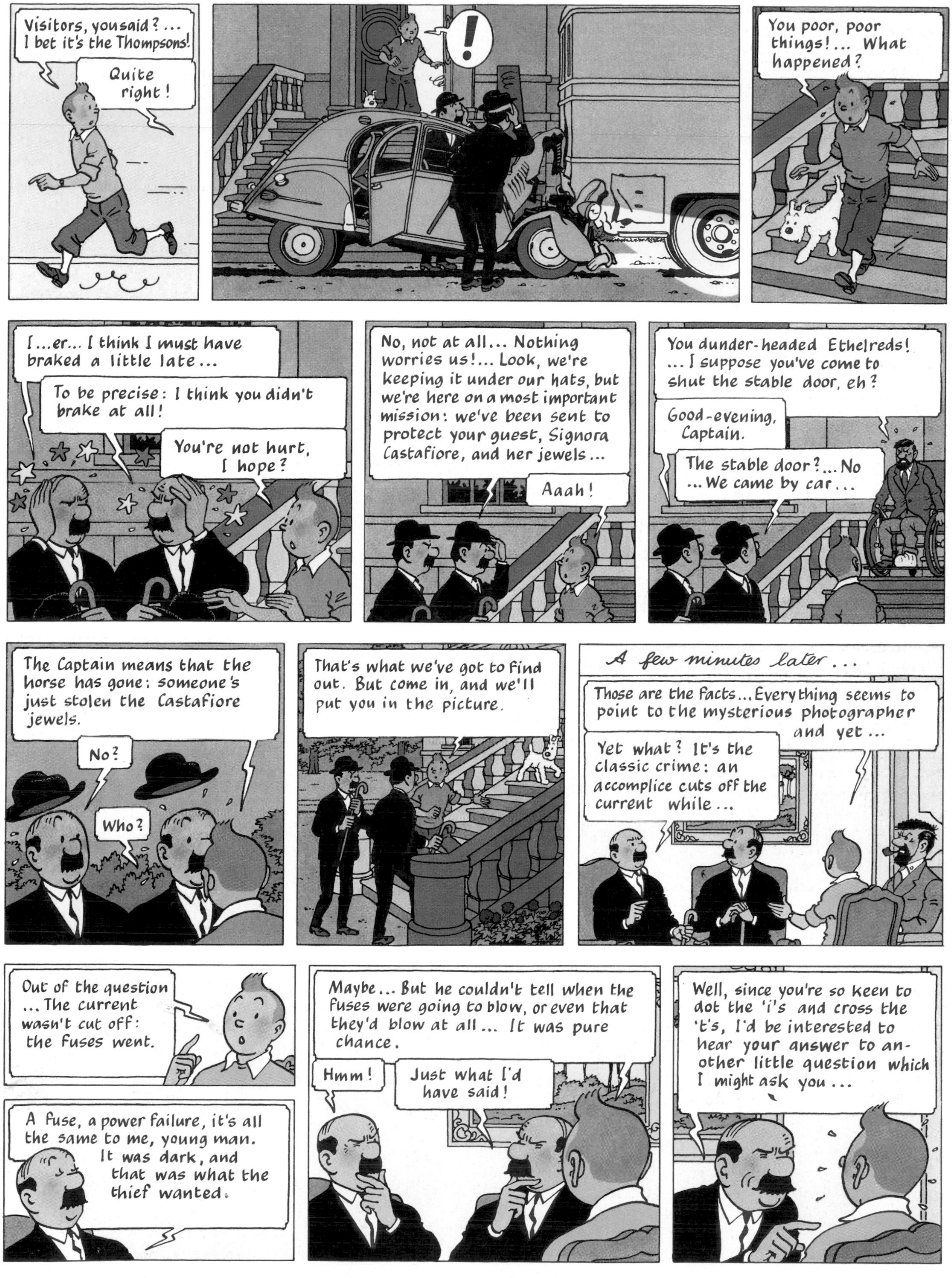

Visitors, you said? ... I bet it's the Thompsons!
Quite right!
!
You poor, poor things! ... What happened?
I ...er... I think I must have braked a little late ...
To be precise: I think you didn't brake at all!
You're not hurt, I hope?
No, not at all... Nothing worries us!... Look, we're keeping it under our hats, but we're here on a most important mission: we've been sent to protect your guest, Signora Castafiore, and her jewels ...
Aaah!
You dunder-headed Ethelreds! ... I suppose you've come to shut the stable door, eh?
Good-evening, Captain.
The stable door? ... No ... We came by car ...
The Captain means that the horse has gone: someone's just stolen the Castafiore jewels.
No?
Who?
That's what we've got to find out. But come in, and we'll put you in the picture.
A few minutes later ...
Those are the facts ... Everything seems to point to the mysterious photographer and yet ...
Yet what? It's the classic crime: an accomplice cuts off the current while ...
Out of the question ... The current wasn't cut off: the fuses went.
A fuse, a power failure, it's all the same to me, young man. It was dark, and that was what the thief wanted.
Maybe ... But he couldn't tell when the fuses were going to blow, or even that they'd blow at all ... It was pure chance.
Hmm!
Just what I'd have said!
Well, since you're so keen to dot the 'i's and cross the 't's, I'd be interested to hear your answer to another little question which I might ask you ...

You say the fuses blew... All right... But did you discover that for yourself? ...

It was Nestor who told me, when he came up from the cellar.

Nestor? ... The butler? ... Aha!

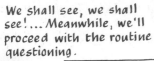
Aha!

Nestor, who once worked for those crooks the Bird brothers ...A good testimonial!

You know perfectly well, when those gangsters were tried the evidence proved that Nestor knew nothing of their activities. Anyway...

Anyway, blistering barnacles, Nestor is absolutely honest, and I forbid you to suspect him!

We shall see, we shall see!...Meanwhile, we'll proceed with the routine questioning.

Very well. Follow me.

Look out, there are cables all over the place.

Yes...

We know!

Thompson and Thomson, certified detectives.

No one is to leave!

And here's Signora Castafiore. I see she's come round.

Ah, Signora Nightingale, the Milanese Castafiore...

Signora!

Charmed!

Madam, we are here to set light to...er, to throw light on the circumstances surrounding your terrible loss...

To be precise ... er ...

Go on, gentlemen.

Just to clear up one point, madam: where were the jewels usually hocked ... I mean locked?

In a drawer in my room, upstairs... Oh my jewels! ... My beautiful jewels! ...

Dead or alive, we shall find them, madam. Leave no stone unturned, that is our policy... Which reminds me: I presume your jewels are fully insured?

Alas, no, gentlemen...

Mr. Swag promised to fix the whole thing up for me ...

Swag? Fix it up?... Fix what? ... Madam, is this some sort of conspiracy?...

No, no gentlemen. Mr. Swag represents an insurance company.

Ah, that's all right... Otherwise...

Yes, otherwise...

Now, your jewels were in a drawer upstairs... Good... Was the drawer locked?

Yes, and the key was hidden in a vase. I fetched it from there earlier on, when I took the case out of the drawer.

The case?... What case was that, madam?

Why, my jewel case of course, the one I...

I... Mamma mia! ... I remember now!

I was sitting here...

There!... There!... What did I tell you?

My jewels! Look! The little darlings!... All here?... Yes!... Oh, I could weep for joy, I'm so pleased to see them!

I really am a feather-brain!... I completely forgot, I'd come downstairs with my jewel-case, when these nice people from television arrived. How too, too hilarious! Ahaha!... What a good laugh!... Don't you agree, gentlemen?

Laugh, madam?... Us, madam? ... We are not amused, madam! ... Good night!

Quite so; we are not amusing!

What is wrong?... Oh dear, what have I done?... Why are they so cross?

Here, your hats!... And mind the cables!

Thank you, we can manage. ... We've told you before: we're not children!

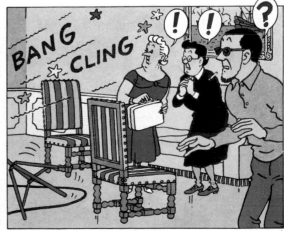

BANG

CLING

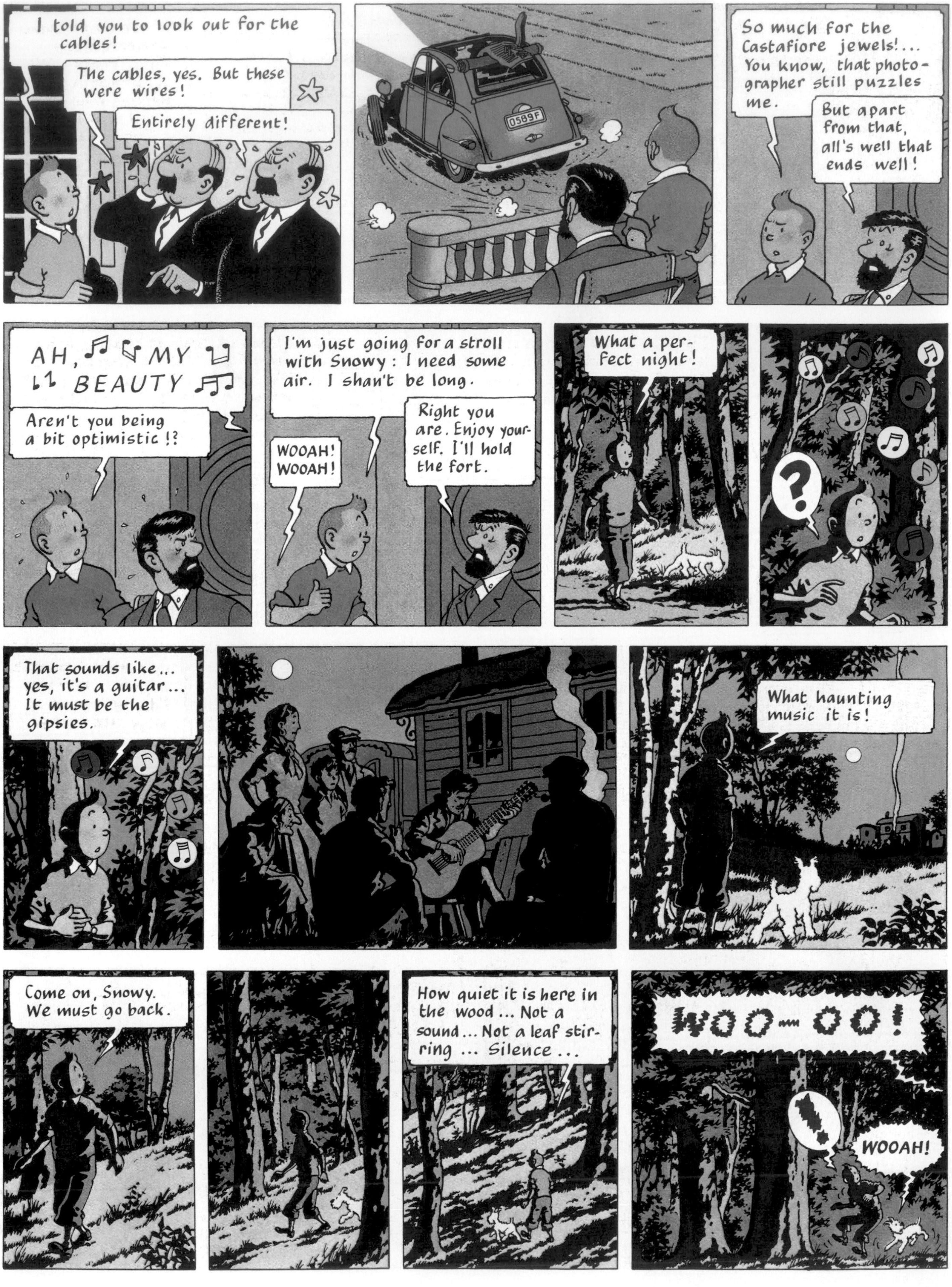

I told you to look out for the cables!
The cables, yes. But these were wires!
Entirely different!
0589F
So much for the Castafiore jewels!... You know, that photographer still puzzles me.
But apart from that, all's well that ends well!
AH, MY BEAUTY
Aren't you being a bit optimistic !?
I'm just going for a stroll with Snowy: I need some air. I shan't be long.
WOOAH! WOOAH!
Right you are. Enjoy yourself. I'll hold the fort.
What a perfect night!
That sounds like... yes, it's a guitar... It must be the gipsies.
What haunting music it is!
Come on, Snowy. We must go back.
How quiet it is here in the wood... Not a sound... Not a leaf stirring ... Silence ...
WOO-OO!
WOOAH!

TU~WOOO

An owl!...Heavens, how it made me jump!

Come on, Snowy. Home!

Three days later...

Yes... yes, I know... I mean ... Yes, it was a wedding... er... my step-sister's cousin ...Yes... Look sir... I'll be with you tomorrow morning ...Yes, yes, definitely... Yes, yes, I promise, sir... Yes, sir... Good-bye, sir.

If you don't come tomorrow, my fine friend, I'll ... blistering barnacles, I don't know what I'll do ...but I won't stand for it!

SLAM

No! I won't stand for it! I tell you: I won't stand for it!

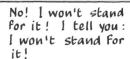

I'll take them to court!... I'll have them locked up!...To make fun of a poor, weak woman!

Mind the step!

I know!... Look at that!...It's shameful!...It's a disgrace!... It's monstrous!...But they won't get away with it, I can tell you! ... Look at it!

TEMPO DI ROMA

LA DIVA E IL PAPPAGALLO
In questo numero alle pagg. 8-9-10

But what's the matter?... It's not at all bad, that photograph...

Not bad!...Not bad!... Is that all you can say? It's horrible, I tell you!

Horrible? I wouldn't say so... In fact, I'd say it was a very good likeness.

That's right!...Defend the cads!...the boors! ... the bumpkins!...Mannerless yokels!...This is the limit!... And it's not just a question of the likeness! ... It's far worse than that!

Worse than that? What do you mean?

41

I mean... I mean that photograph was taken here by a reporter from the "Tempo", and he got in without a soul knowing!... You let people use this house like a hotel!

What? That photographer...

Yes, that photographer, the one who got away in the dark... Oh, it's too bad! I said to that "Tempo" riff-raff: "You've dared to say that I weigh fourteen stone!... Very well: no more photographs, no more interviews!... You can tell your reporters I never want to see their faces again!"

And now by some diabolical trick they've managed to run a whole feature!... And all because of you! It's all your fault!

My fault?!...

Of course it is!... If you were more particular about the people who invite themselves in... If you didn't open your door to every Tom, Dick and Harry, this would never have happened!... And you! Wagner! I want a word with you!

So you've come back, Mister Wagner!... Where have you been? ... And who gave you permission to go out?... You have work to do, Mr. Wagner; scales, Mr. Wagner!

But...

Silence!... Your playing is careless, Mr. Wagner!...Two wrong notes yesterday!...In future I want to hear you practising all day long. Is that clear?

Yes, signora...
No, signora...
Yes, signora.

And you, Irma!... Have you found your little gold scissors yet?... Obviously not!... What's got into you, girl?

Me, madame?

D O N G

Yes, you Irma!... And go and see who that is, instead of gawking like an idiot!

Hello, girlie!

'Morning, Duchess!... How goes it? ... All O.K.?... And your hubby-to-be? He all right?... Fine!...Well, here we are: I've brought you a dinky little insurance policy...

I'm so sorry, Mr. Sag!...You're too late!... The early bird catches the worm, Mr. Sag!

Come off it! You're joking!

Don't try to argue, Mr. Sag... I shall take care of my own jewels, Mr. Sag!... Good morning, Mr. Sag.

SLAM

?

This is the end!

Ah, dear lady. It's quite extraordinary; I just found this magazine on the floor ... And guess whose charming likeness adorns the cover ... Look!

I know, Professor Candyfloss! I know!... And kindly refrain from calling it a likeness!

Isn't it?...A most striking resemblance. ...As for the parrot...

... he looks as if he's enjoying the joke ... But wait ...

That isn't all... Wait, there are some more pages inside. Now, let me see...

Ah, Chester!

So you deign to come? It's ten minutes since the bell rang! I suppose you think I'm here to answer the door for you!

Let's see now...

But ...

One moment, dear lady... I think I've got it... Yes, here we are...

Look...?!

But I could have sworn ...

The days go by...

Scales! scales! scales! scales!

... until one morning ...

Scales! scales!

MERCY! MY JEWELS!   MURDER!   MY EMERALD!

There she goes!... She's lost her geegaws again.

You hear?

Yes, yes...don't worry: she'll find them in a minute or two.

THUMP

Someone's missed that step again!

43

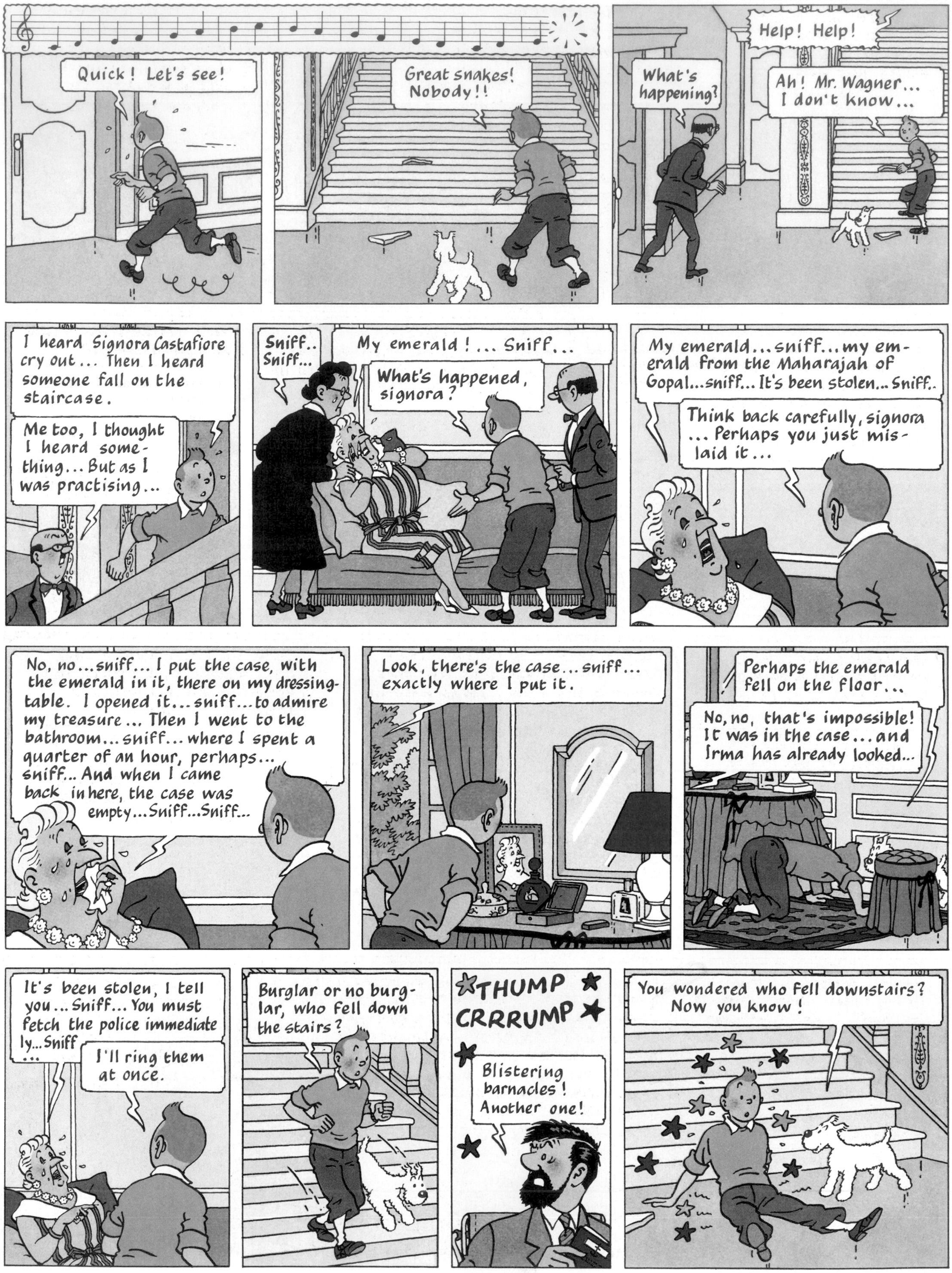
Quick! Let's see!
Great snakes! Nobody!!
Help! Help!
What's happening?
Ah! Mr. Wagner... I don't know...
I heard Signora Castafiore cry out... Then I heard someone fall on the staircase.
Me too, I thought I heard something... But as I was practising...
Sniff.. Sniff...
My emerald!... Sniff...
What's happened, signora?
My emerald... sniff... my emerald from the Maharajah of Gopal...sniff... It's been stolen... Sniff..
Think back carefully, signora ... Perhaps you just mislaid it...
No, no...sniff... I put the case, with the emerald in it, there on my dressing-table. I opened it... sniff... to admire my treasure... Then I went to the bathroom... sniff... where I spent a quarter of an hour, perhaps... sniff... And when I came back in here, the case was empty...Sniff...Sniff...
Look, there's the case... sniff... exactly where I put it.
Perhaps the emerald fell on the floor...
No, no, that's impossible! It was in the case... and Irma has already looked...
It's been stolen, I tell you... Sniff... You must fetch the police immediately...Sniff...
I'll ring them at once.
Burglar or no burglar, who fell down the stairs?
THUMP
CRRRUMP
Blistering barnacles! Another one!
You wondered who fell downstairs? Now you know!

Unless I'm very much mistaken, it was the thief who fell on the stairs just now.

Hello? Yes this is me... Yes, with a 'p', as in Philadelphia ... Good mor... What... A robbery?!... An emerald!?! But ...I... Look... Signora Castafiore ...She's quite sure, isn't she; it really has been stolen this time?

A good question.

Yes, I'm afraid it has.

Good...That's lucky for her. I don't mind telling you, if she'd got us up to Marlinspike on another wild goose chase we wouldn't have come.

Definitely not!

Half an hour later ...

In a nutshell... If the theft was committed by someone in the house, then there are only six suspects: Irma, Wagner, Nestor, Calculus, Tintin, and of course you yourself, Captain.

Are you suggesting...!?

Wait!... Three on our list can be ruled straight out: you, because you couldn't have gone upstairs in your wheelchair; Tintin, who was with you; and Wagner: he was playing the piano in the maritime gallery.

If you can call it playing ...

That leaves Irma, Nestor, and the Professor.

One of those three a criminal?... You must be crazy!

And so, with your permission, we will question each of them separately, in private.

All right. I'll send Nestor in. But you're wasting your time.

Where was I?... In the garden, near Professor Calculus who was pruning his roses...I was watering the begonias when I heard Signora Castafiore shouting... I looked up at the windows...

Oho! You admit you could see the windows from where you were?

Certainly, sir... Then, as the cries continued, I dropped my watering can and hastened towards the house...

You were in a hurry to reach the house, eh?... That is all. Please ask the Captain to send in Irma.

Sniff... I was busy sewing in my room... sniff... Suddenly...sniff...I heard madame calling out...sniff...I ran to her room...sniff...just in time...sniff...to catch her in my arms... sniff... as she fainted ... sniff...

Aha!

Your mistress has told us she spent about a quarter of an hour in the bathroom. In short, knowing her habits, you would have had an opportunity to enter her room, without any noise, and slip out with the emerald ... or drop it from the window to an accomplice...To Nestor, for instance!...Come on! Confess!

EEEEEEEEK!

Help!

Tintin! Save me!

Beasts! YEOW! OW!

?! !

Beasts! Beasts! Beasts!

Irma! Irma! What's the matter?...Stop!

They...sniff...they accused me...sniff...of stealing...sniff...madame's emerald...I...sniff...who have never...sniff...taken a pin...sniff...which didn't belong to me...sniff...In fact...sniff...It was I...sniff..who had my little scissors stolen...sniff...and my beautiful silver thimble...And they dare accuse me...sniff...those wicked men!

BOO-HOO-HOOO!

Is that true? Did you really accuse her?

Er...well...I...sort of... You see, it's a trick that comes off some-times.

Just a slight mishap. An occupational hazard... Will you send in Calculus?

Certainly. But if I were you, I'd try some other method.

Professor, is it true that Nestor was near you when Signora Castafiore first cried out?

Not at all! It's not in the least inconvenient. I've been told about the theft, and I am heart-broken for the dear lady, heart-broken.

Yes...well...er...To get back to my question, Professor...

I thought of that at once, of course... And I'd already come to certain conclusions before you sent for me.

No! no! no! I won't stand for it!

Of course, it's only a matter of simple direction find-ing; watch my pendulum.

?

Oh, so there you are!

It's swinging to the south-east. In fact it's pointing...

What is this I hear?... You had the effrontery to accuse Irma?... My honest Irma!... I won't stand for it! To attack a poor, weak woman! I shall complain to the United Nations!

... in the direction of the gipsy camp.

And if Irma gives in her notice, as she may well after such an insult, will you find me a new maid? ...And what about the higher wages the new girl will want: will you pay those? ... I tell you, if you don't apologize to Irma...

... I leave this house immediately. I shall tell the Captain!

You see? It points south-east.

Now... where were we?...

You understand, I'm not accusing anyone. It's simply that my pendulum indicates the direction of their camp.

A camp? What are you talking about?

Excuse me! I must stop you there!...They are real gipsies. I've seen them as clearly as I see you!

I say, your friend Calculus, is he a bit...er, you know? He keeps on talking about a gipsy encampment.

Yes, that's right. There's a Romany camp quite close.

Is that true?... Why didn't you say so before?...They're the villains, without a shadow of doubt!

But look here, what proof have you?

Proof? We shall find it!...Those sort of people are always thieving! There's no time to be lost: take us to their camp.

All right, I will. But you've no right to suspect them just because they're gipsies.

I'll be surprised if they're still there. Having done the job, they'll have bolted.

I don't think so!

Where's the camp?

OH!

Well?

They... they've gone!...But I saw them only last night...

What did I tell you? They've done a bunk.

They won't have got far.

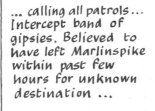

... calling all patrols... Intercept band of gipsies. Believed to have left Marlinspike within past few hours for unknown destination ...

"Investigation into the theft of the Castafiore emerald continues"... etc. etc... Ah! "The gipsies who were camping near Marlinspike at the time of the robbery have been assisting the police in their inquir... ies. A headquarters spokesman refused to comment on the affair"... There!

Those poor things ... And I'm absolutely certain they are innocent.

Me too. I'd stake my life on it ... but...

Tintin! Captain! My dear friends! ... A sensational discovery! ... Sen-sa-tion-al! ... I've just invented a television set!

You old pioneer!

Colour television, of course! The other day, looking at all those sets, I thought to myself: what a pity the pictures are only in black and white!

You know, someone has already...

Not at all, it's just a question of know-how. Now listen carefully... The people you see on the little screen are in black and white, aren't they? But in the studio?... What about that?

The studio?

Er...

I don't need to tell you... In the studio the subjects are all in colour... Well, the purpose of my apparatus is to restore those colours!...How?...How?... Well, roughly speaking, by colour filters inserted between an ordinary television set and a special screen. I call it "Super-Calcacolor."

But that's brilliant!

You think so?... In all modesty I must say my own comment would be: brilliant! But you shall judge my invention for yourselves. Tonight they have that famous programme "Scanorama"... Will you join me?

That evening ...

Now my friends, hold your breath!... This is an historic moment!

Tonight... BING ... Scanorama... BONG... your look at life... DONG

...brings the big news of three continents to your fireside. Our roving cameras give you a close-up of...

...the 21st Taschist Party Congress at Szohõd, the secret life of the Abominable Snowman, and the jewel robbery at Marlinspike...

Well, I'll be...

What a coincidence!

How very strange!

At the 21st Taschist Party Congress at Szohôd, Marshal Kûrvi-Tasch, in an exceptionally violent speech...

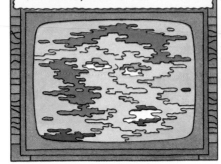

The picture isn't absolutely clear, but I can adjust it...

DIGADOG DAGADIGADUG DOGODOGDOG DAGODAGODAGODUG DIGADIGDUG

That's better, isn't it?

It's the sound, now!

All right, eh? The sound! ...Thundering typhoons, adjust the sound!

CRACK

Oh dear!... A valve has gone!... It won't take long to replace...

Ten minutes later...

There! That's done it!

...summary of the facts. As you know, the famous Italian singer Bianca Castafiore is staying in this country...

Ah, ♪ my beauty ♫ ♪ past compare ♩ ♪ ♪

Is that me? Oh, how horrible!

At historic Marlinspike Hall, the prima donna was the victim of a daring robbery. A magnificent emerald vanished . . . mysteriously!

Today a Scanorama reporter went down to Marlinspike and spoke to the officers in charge of the case. Over to Thompson and Thomson...

No, our lips are sealed. We can't tell you whom we suspect, but it isn't anyone in the house. Mum's the word, you know.

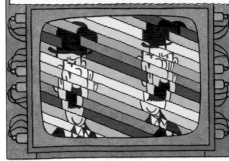

Yes, dumb's the word, that's our motto. So we're not allowed to tell you about the gipsies, though we suspected them from the start...

Especially after they cleft their lamp...er...left their camp, the morning after the robbery. But we soon ran them to earth, and then when we searched their caravans we made a startling discovery!

49

Not only did we discover a pair of scissors belonging to Signora Casta-fiore's maid, but in one of their caravans...

...we found a messed-up flunkey ...er...a dressed-up monkey. Ob-viously, the emerald could only have been stolen by a man climb-ing the wall: in fact, a man of remarkable agility...And that man has been found: the monkey! Of course the whole bunch...

...denied it furiously. The scissors had been 'found' by a little girl. As for the monkey, he'd never been out of his cage.

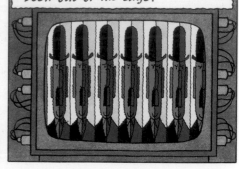

So that's how things stand ... but we're keeping it under our hats, of course. All we have to do now is recover the emerald...

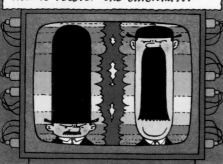

And for a couple of master-minds like you, gentlemen, that will be child's play...Thank you for putting us so clearly in the picture.

Now we turn from the excitement and suspense of a police investigat-ion to another burning topic that is hitting today's headlines...

Oh no! That's enough!

Stop! My eyes are simply streaming!

Enough! Enough!

Naturally, it isn't entirely perfect yet, but ...

My eyeballs are doing the shimmy!

I'm seeing six of everything!

Me too!

The next morning...

Poor gipsies!... I'm still convinced they're innocent... I've had another look at the wall: even a monkey climbing would have left some trace, but there wasn't a sign. What then?

Hello! There's Mr. Wagner go-ing into the village, on Nestor's old bike.

He must have got permission to leave his piano. Now's our chance, Snowy...

We'll go back in-doors... and we'll be spared that piano for a change!

?

Surely I didn't imagine it... I just saw Mr. Wagner going off on his bike ...So who can be playing the piano?

What have you found, Snowy?

Wooah! Wooah!

Oho! Someone's hidden a ladder down here... Better and better!... Well, since it's here, we'll make use of it.

He won't be back yet... Up we go!

!?

?

Great snakes!

A battery tape-recorder! It's a playback of his own scales! But what's it all in aid of? ...

Why? Why?... Well, Mr. Wagner, we're going to find out! First, I must be quick and put the ladder back.

There!

Hide yourself somewhere, Snowy, and don't make a sound.

Wooah!

And now, maestro, I'm ready for you!

No one about: I'll risk it...

Can I give you a hand, Mr. Wagner?

No thanks, I can manage.

H-h-how did you get in here?

The same way as you, Mr. Wagner... But do put down the ladder...

I...er... I do it to get a little exercise... Original, don't you think?

Very! And the tape-recorder... for the same purpose, eh?

Oh, yes, the tape-recorder...Look, you must promise not to tell Signora Castafiore. I worked out a plan so I could get some fresh air from time to time... She keeps me at the piano all day long, you know, and ...

Fresh air? Village air, I believe, Mr. Wagner.

Oh, so you know! Then I'd better tell you everything...

IRMAA!... Oh, have you seen Irma?

Now I'm in for it! I forgot to lock the door!

Irma? No, signora.

Thank you... But... Well, Mr. Wagner, what about your scales?

My s-s-scales, s-s-signora?...

But he's playing them, signora... as you can hear.

Of course... So he is... I wasn't thinking. Forgive me!

Silly me!... so absent-minded!

Thanks...But why did you save me from her?

I wanted to get you alone ...Now, sit down at the piano: it's safer...Then talk!

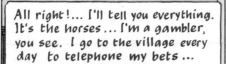

All right!... I'll tell you everything. It's the horses...I'm a gambler, you see. I go to the village every day to telephone my bets...

Hmm!

Is that so?...Still, you weren't in the village when the emerald was stolen...when some unknown person fell down the stairs...It was you, wasn't it?

Yes, it was I.

I'd been up to the attic...and on my way down I heard Signora Castafiore cry out...I hurried to get back to my piano, and missed the step.

Why were you in the attic?

Well, on a number of evenings I thought I heard someone walking about up there...at dusk...like the signora did on the night we arrived. In the end I decided to get to the bottom of it...

Why didn't you simply ask us?

I didn't want to make a fool of myself, if it was only a false alarm...Anyway, I didn't find anything.

One last point, Mr. Wagner. The day after you came, I found your footprints under Signora Castafiore's window...

Golly, how some people do love to talk!

Yes...it's quite possible. After that incident during the night I went round there, to make sure no one could have climbed the ivy.

Good...That's all the explanation I need.

No, I don't think Wagner stole the emerald: he seems to be telling the truth..Well, now I've got to find the real culprit!

In any case, I'll visit the attic tonight. We must follow every lead...Coming, Snowy?

Ah... at last!

At nightfall...

Ssh!

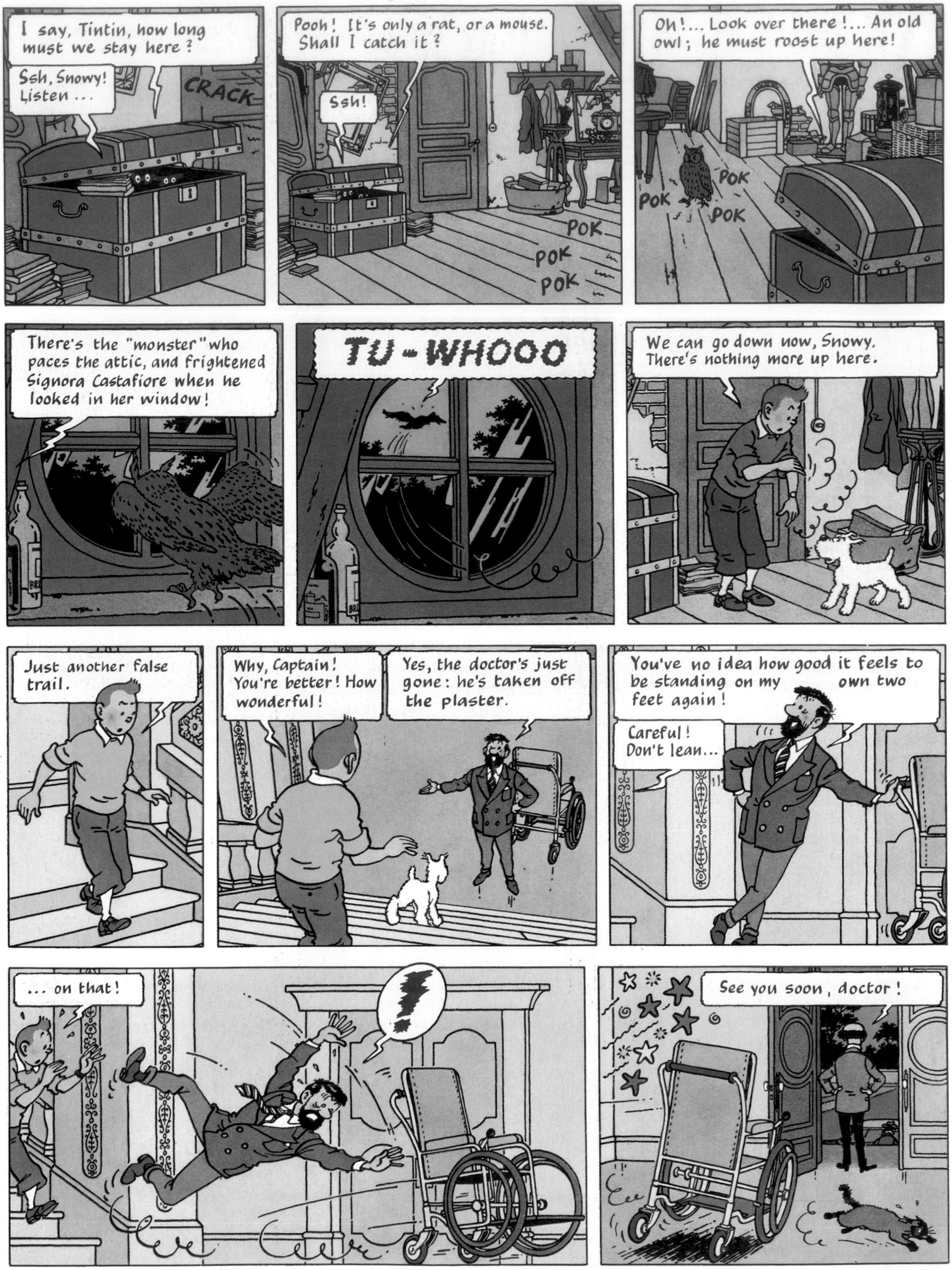
I say, Tintin, how long must we stay here?
Ssh, Snowy! Listen ...
CRACK
Pooh! It's only a rat, or a mouse. Shall I catch it?
Ssh!
POK
POK
POK
Oh!... Look over there!... An old owl; he must roost up here!
POK
POK
POK
There's the "monster" who paces the attic, and frightened Signora Castafiore when he looked in her window!
TU-WHOOO
We can go down now, Snowy. There's nothing more up here.
Just another false trail.
Why, Captain! You're better! How wonderful!
Yes, the doctor's just gone: he's taken off the plaster.
You've no idea how good it feels to be standing on my own two feet again!
Careful! Don't lean...
... on that!
!
See you soon, doctor!

Great snakes! What's going to happen?

One day I really must turn out the clutter in this car!

What was it?... What happened?

What happened? What was it? ...

My dear Captain Padlock... Why, you're up!... I'm so glad.

Thanks!

It grieves me to cloud your happiness, but I have sad news for you: I must leave you tomorrow.

No!... Not really? It can't be true!

Alas, dear friend! They are clamouring for me at La Scala in Milan: a farewell performance in Rossini before I leave for the States.

I'm terribly upset ...I'm shattered.. You won't change your mind?

You're an angel, trying to keep me here, but I already have my tickets.

Ah!

She's going! She's going!

She's go-go-go-going away ♪♫ Hip hip hip hooray! This is my lucky day!

She's go...guo...gug'!...Ta-ra-ra-er... um...yes... H'mm.

... This is my lucky day! ... My wheelchair's going away!

The big baby!

Come along in. A drink will soon put you right.

The moment of departure comes ...

Goodbye, signora... Bon voyage!

Goodbye, dear Captain Hatbox! Thank you again for your charming hospitality... It grieves me so to leave you, but I give you my promise: I'll be back!

I... I'm sure you will!

As for my emerald... sniff...sniff... the moment you have any news...

Yes, yes, I'll let you know at once, never fear...

Dear lady, I beg you to accept these humble roses, the first of a new variety I have created... I have ventured to give them your beautiful name, "Bianca"!

What a sweet idea!

They are exquisite! ... Ex-x-x-quisite! And what perfume! Smell them, Captain Stockpot!

No, thank you!

Dear Professor, let me embrace you!

SMACK

Now I simply must go...

Yes...yes, you really must...Goodbye!

Arrivederci! Take care of Iago!

Don't you worry!

Goodbye, dear lady...

Come back soon!!

MERCY, MY JEWELS!

Oh, sir!...Sir!...The signora has forgotten this!

Mercy! her jewels!

Thank you, Hector! ...As a special favour, I'll send you a signed photograph.

70V14

This time they've really gone... It's all over! Finished! ...No more scales! No more "Mercy! my jewels!"

MERCY! MY JEWELS!

!

So it's you, clever dick! If you value your feathers, I advise you to put on another record!

CRO!

BILLIONS OF BLISTERING BARNACLES! SHUT UP WHEN I'M TALKING!

Three days later...

Yes...yes...yes, I know... It isn't my fault... What? ... No, it isn't your fault either... Yes... It was the band annual outing ...Then I had a touch of 'flu, and...When?...To-morrow?...'Fraid that's impossible ...Maybe the beginning of next week ...

Just wait till I get my hands on you, Mr. Bolt...Then you'll hear a thing or two!

SLAM

Can't understand these folks...always in a hurry...Give themselves high blood pressure, that's what they'll do.

Just what I say, Arthur.

Have you seen this in the 'Daily Reporter'? It's about ...

...old Castorolli. Yes, I read it.

Nightingale
with a Broken Heart

MILAN, TUESDAY

'Triumph . . . superlative . . . sublime . . . unforgettable,' proclaims the Italian press. At La Scala last night the divine Castafiore bid farewell to Europe. An ecstatic audience acclaimed her overwhelming performance in Rossini's LA GAZZA LADRA.

Time and again a delirious house recalled their idol. Fifteen curtains! Bravo! Bravissimo! But can the plaudits of admirers mend a broken heart? For the nightingale still mourns the loss of her most precious jewel.

And have we heard the last of the Castafiore emerald? Not so. Police investigations continue in the Marlinspike area. Was a monkey used to spirit away the jewel, magnificent gift of the Maharajah of Gopal? No comment, say detectives, but suspicion weighs heavily upon local gipsies. And still no sign of the emerald.

From Italy, the Milanese nightingale wings her way tonight

Still that ridiculous idea of a thieving monkey. Whoever heard of an animal so well trained that it goes straight to a particular object?

Talking of animals, d'you know what that builder said?

But...but... Great snakes!... Why not??

Why not what?

Where are you going? Where in the world ...

I'll be back in a minute!

Wooah! Wooah!

I wonder what's got into him?

Tell me, Captain, is there any message you'd like to send to Signora Castafiore?

A message?... Me?... For Castafiore?

No, a message!... I forgot to tell you, I'm leaving today for Milan: I'm going there to demonstrate my Super-Calcacolor to the International Television Congress. Naturally, I shall call upon our charming friend.

Oh? Well, tell her whatever you like: but for pity's sake, don't invite her back to Marlinspike!

That's very kind: I'll tell her. She'll certainly be touched by your invitation...

Captain! Captain!

Now what?... Has he set the house on fire?

Is there a woodman anywhere near?

A woodman?... Yes, Charlie Sawyer, in the village... But why?

Thanks!... Oh, I almost forgot... Ring up the Thompsons... Tell them to come here as soon as possible: about the emerald.

About the emerald?... What?...

Later!... And remember to telephone, won't you?

But Tintin, look here...

Half an hour later...

We've only come as a special flavour... er, savour... er, well, so far as we're concerned, there's absolutely nothing Tintin can add to the case. Once and for all, the job was done by the gipsies, with the help of their monkey.

It's as clear as day to us, eh Thompson?

To be precise: dear as clay. That's my opinion and I'm stuck with it!

There's only one thing Tintin can tell us: where the emerald is hidden.

And if you'll come with me, gentlemen, I will do precisely that!

You?!

No?!

Yes?!

You've discovered where the gipsies have hidden the emerald ?

The gipsies haven't hidden anything.

Look up there... That's where you'll find the key to the whole mystery!

There ?

Up where ?

Yes, where up there ?

Up there, in that poplar...

That poplar?... All I can see is a nest.

Yes, but it's a magpie's nest, Captain.

What ? You mean to say...

?

That a magpie stole the emerald : yes, I'd bet my life on it.

Thundering typhoons ! And you borrowed that kit from old man Sawyer to climb up to the nest ...

Exactly!

For heaven's sake be careful, Tintin!

I will!

CHAK-CHAK!

Tintin! Do please watch your step!

Don't worry I'm ...

CRACK...

Look out for the dead branch!

CRACK

No damage done!...What about you? Have you found anything?

Yes, and how! I've got Irma's thimble ...

AND THE EMERALD! HERE'S THE EMERALD!!

Some bits of glass... a marble... and a monocle...That's the lot... I'm coming down.

Chak-chak

Thief!

Wonderful!... Tintin, you're a genius!...But what on earth suddenly made you think of a magpie?

Do you remember the name of the opera they mentioned in the paper?

I don't know... "Pizza" or "Ragazza"...or something ...

"La Gazza Ladra"... in other words, The Thieving Magpie! Then the light dawned!

I thought to myself: "There's a 'gazza ladra' somewhere around... But where? ... What about the spot where Miarka found the scissors? They must have fallen from the robber's hiding-place." ...So I ran to look, and there was the nest!... Well, that clears the gipsies!

Just our luck! The one time we manage to catch the culprits they turn out to be innocent! It's really too bad of them!

You'd think they'd done it on purpose!

Anyway, thanks to us, the emerald has turned up. And all we have to do is to return it to Signora Castafiore.

You know, Cuthbert Calculus is just leaving for Milan. Couldn't we give him the jewel?

Definitely not! We and we alone must restore the emerald: we are in beauty downed! ...

As you like: here it is.

You know, what pleases me is the relief for the gipsies. They'll be completely cleared of suspicion now.

It's a sight for sore eyes...

To be precise, I'd say...

? ? OH!

What are you doing?

It's...er...it's the... It's the emerald...it fell on the grass...and the grass is green...

As green as grass!

That's rich!... Yes, that's rich!... Oh, it's marvellous!

It could happen to anybody...

Wooah! Wooah! Here's your brandy-ball!

There! And hang on to it, this time!

Trust me!

A few minutes later...

Goodbye, my friends. I'm just off... Is there any message for Signora Castafiore?

Yes, indeed!

Wonderful news! You can tell her that her emerald has been found ...by Tintin!

Oh no! I'm flying: it's so much quicker.

I said the Castafiore emerald has been found! The em-er-ald!

THE EMERALD!!

Certainly not... I never do... I make it a point of honour to declare everything at the customs... Goodbye.

It's all right, Captain...Calm down! All we have to do is to send a telegram to Signora Castafiore.

I won't forget to give her your invitation...

We're off now... taking the mule to Japan...er, making the gruel...faking the jewel... Anyway, goodbye, Captain.

Goodbye! Goodbye!

Goodbye! And thanks for trying to help with the case.

Have you got the emerald?

No, you've got it!

Excuse me, I gave it to you!

You certainly did not!...

Next morning...

What a glorious walk... Not a cloud in the sky! ... Perfect peace! ... Wonderful!...

Ah, there you are! Look here!

Why?... What's happened? ...Don't tell me SHE's come back!

Look! Mr. Bolt has been to mend the step.

That's wonderful!...Ah, he's put a board across it: to give the mortar time to set. I expect he warned you.

No, he didn't. But it's quite obvious...

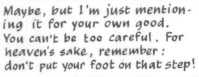

Maybe, but I'm just mentioning it for your own good. You can't be too careful. For heaven's sake, remember: don't put your foot on that step!

Right, Captain.

Indeed, sir.

For the next few days you must step over... like tha-a-at! You understand?

Yes, Captain.

Very good, sir.

You see? It's perfectly easy. You just have to think what you're doing...

DONG

Hello... Who's that?

It's me again... I forgot to tell you...

Ah, Mr. Bolt! It was nice of you to come...

TU-WHOO

That's a real shame! I just popped back to say, wait a day or two before using that step... Too bad: a lovely bit of marble, that was!

Chak-chak

Blistering barnacles, that's the end!

HERGÉ

62